CW00350583

Mortem

By Russell Mc Dougall

The monsters of the mind are far worse than those that exist. Fear, doubt and hate have hamstrung more people than beasts ever have.

CHRISTOPHER PAOLINI, Brisingr

Glencoe Scotland 1504

Now I need to explain, with detail, a place to you. It's very important you remember this place in your mind for this glen will reshape the world as we know it!

The sky bright white with haze bursting and blending from whites to hazy greys, bulging with moisture and rain. A slim waterfall slides down the perfect, nature cut, gorge out the Scottish countryside. Rocks rise like massive stone pancakes unevenly stacked up in cartoon like columns. The water breaks down on these, creating upside-down u shapes as part of nature's beauty. To the left of the fall a glowing purple field of brilliance as the purple shades of the Scottish heather melts into the undergrowth and grass, surrounding to create an almost pearlescent effect. Alongside the bottom of the waterfall it spills into a zig zagging stream, colliding past the year-old debris of rocks that have fallen from the sheer cliff tops, above the water now running as clear and clean as the air surrounding the stream. Rocks, varying in size, all cracked like circuitry and large patches of dark green moss, intruding from corner and gaps like infection. Although the rocks are grey in nature, glimmering lines of quartz are running through most, as if they have been cut open like a scone buttered and put back together. To the right a thousand shades of green climbing up diagonally, forming a web of green beauty. Nature at its best. To stand back and look at the whole scene from afar, the effect of liquid clouds running down a mountain can be a fair assessment. The rain collects enmasse on the hill side and forms into a grey mist getting deeper in colour by the minute. The mass moves down into the glen and implodes with magnitude drenching every inch of the scenery. Leaves suddenly no longer calm, still, motionless shelves and have become an array of vibrating glimmers of dew. The ground in between the rocks and heather becomes a sludge between solid and slime, a paste of mud, the kind that always traps in your shoes, the kind that spatters up your leg as soon as you even step into it. Behind the entire vista lies a dark forest dense and thick, leaves merging into each other after years of knitting together. The barks thick and proud, almost alive, as their glorious marking emphasize time and wear, nothing uniform except the tall looming height looking deep into the forest. It looks like it could go on forever, a mass of twigs and overgrowth combined into a city sized spider web. In the distance of the web like wood, deep into the wood, lights appear in the depth flickering. In a far distance their colour - orange in nature, they start out with two or three, but they keep increasing. First five, then twenty, now hundreds. Muffled shouts in the distance signify how far away they are almost like faint echoes dripping through trees. A closer sound is there, but what is it? Not like shouting or screaming, more physical and motion filled.

THUD, a foot slams into the soft mud and freeze frames around it, the boot is leather and halfway up to the shin, the face buckled up with shining silver clips and tightly sealed like a trusted-up bit of beef. The front of the shoe pointed just enough not to be feminine. As time stands still around this sudden foot, beads of water, containing convex expanses of the world around them, rise from the mud and join the air in a collection of fancy Christmas like bobbles.

There is a sound, almost like a squelch in reverse and an increasing gentle wind noise. That wind noise channels into a fast pulse, and the boot accelerates at an incredible pace, followed by another. The owner of these boots moves in a blur like motion directly into the glen, leaving a wind of splashing water and leaves. Combined into an after following of haze, the figure slams to an almost animated stop to reveal himself. A tall figure, skinny in a muscular way, tightly packed muscle like the kind of muscle you see on a well walked Jack Russell. Rather than big and bulky like that of a steroid abuser. The metal clasped boots lead on to thick woven socks. Then to colored legs with a dusting of light hair. Atop this, a pristine clean red, blue and green kilt, latched through a pin shaped like a small silver knife. On the upper muscular body, a smooth cotton loose-fitting traditional Scottish shirt, light cream in colour with black tassels hanging from a neat zig zag of intricate leather lace. Now, the face thin and angular with a proud jaw, light hair fixed back into a perfect brushed ponytail down to shoulder length. Eyes deep black with the appearance of no colour surrounding the pupil, glare fiercely, but at the same time relaxed lips cold colored red, like when you have braced a storm and your lips lose colour. Skin white and pale with a cleanliness about it, not a hair or mole out of place. The figure smiles, revealing an evil demonic smile, and two small pointed teeth. He looks into the forest of glowing lights and lets out a snigger.

As he looks back at the woods, he turns to move up the gorge, in a leap like motion. Suddenly The world turns yellow for minute. A whipping speed of metal, iron metal propels through the picture scene, as a large metal spiked pole, hurtles down and slices through the figures shoulder pinning him to a wooden stump. The pole has an iron rust look to it and the end of the pole bent into an upside U, quite clearly to prevent escape. You must understand for a human being to throw this from range, and not inflict damage of any kind to many creatures, but this item has fallen gaining momentum from a great height. Now trapped, the strange figure lets out a scream of anguish and light hissing growl at the same time. Blood, dark instead of rich red, explodes out of the wound betraying the beautiful scenery with its splatter. The now prone figure growls a second time and looks up to see a tall, well-built man with a warm red ginger beard and hair looking down at him and wearing the same kilt as the figure.

"CCCCOOOOOPPPPPPEEEERRRR"

a strong voice bellows from the man looking down at him. Cooper looks at the metal pole pinning him down, looking for escape he then looks back at the woods. As the lights are growing bigger and beginning to flicker, he looks back to the bearded man. He has now been joined by twenty more men fitting the same description as the first, all holding flame ended torches. It became self-evident to Cooper that those flickering lights in the wood, were hundreds of angry flaming torches. He looked around weighing at his options, there were not many. He let out another growl of pain and anger, almost a hint of disappointment that he could be cornered and outsmarted this way, he took one more futile twist and tug of the pole as the torches got closer and closer.

Chapter 2 Kevin

Edinburgh 1999

Kevin was tall and skinny, with the frame of an animated stick man, barely enough meat to satisfy a hungry cannibal. His clothes, worn and tired, a collection of stains and scuff marks from days of not changing. His jeans, frayed at the bottom without a single solid edge, just a length of hanging fabric hair. His top, branding the name Nike, grey with a large hood and large pocket on the stomach region, also scuffed in a way only two or three days of non-washing can create. Under the mass of hanging hairy jeans, he wore a pair of light brown Rockport shoes, these in this time were quite an expensive pair of shoes, not really fitting the rest of Kevin's outfit, but he had been very fortunate to find them thrown out in an office car park in Leith.

Kevin's face, pale with a yellow grey tinge, had the nicotine staining of a repetitive smoker and abuser. His hair matted and greasy, cheeks sunken and thin gave his face a skeletal appearance.

Kevin had had trouble all through his life, he started smoking cannabis in pipes at second year of school and had been smoking cigarettes since age nine. He left school at the age of fifteen and started smoking heroin seven months later. His father was also a heroin abuser. Kevin had witnessed it his whole life and now his glorious father figure was serving fifteen years in Polmont prison for armed robbery of a Morningside post office. Somehow his gun had gone off and hit a ceiling tile, sixty-seven-year-old women then had a heart attack and died. So, before he even left the place ironically committed armed robbery and manslaughter in one go. The judge stated if I could, I would throw away the key, but I am bind by legal code and you will serve the maximum - I can issue you ….

Kevin was left with his mother who was mentally unstable. When Kevin was at the age of nine, she hung her two cats, then slit her wrists and was immediately sectioned in the Royal Edinburgh hospital for the mentally ill. So, Kevin has had a rough time, is it a wonder he made it this far?

Kevin sits in a doorway just to the left of the Edinburgh university Morningside campus, squeezed length ways wrapped in his Henry jacket. The cold was creeping close to his chest as he struggles to put his brittle dry skinny fingers into his jean pocket, to pull out a crumpled sorry excuse for a cigarette and a green lighter. He straightens it out and places it in his mouth and lights it, a long pull of the poison into his lungs, a deep pause in his face and then a release and a sigh. In his head a million voices of failure and regret. The heroin and alcohol are the only things that dull these voices. The Most recent voice, his aunt, that took him in at nine to prevent him from going in care.

"Kevin, you are a worthless little cunt, I needed that money. You steal everything but, this was the one line you hadn't ever crossed. You're leaving, I no longer care. If I ever see you at my door again I will fuckin kill you. Ashley is like your little sister; how could you have done this to her? ...."

his aunt says, between angry sobs.

With that, Kevin had turned his back and not returned. That was two days ago, he left all his stuff and headed away because what he had done was the worst! He had stolen his aunts ten-year-old daughter's money to buy skag. So, his aunt was displeased to say the least so now Kevin had reached the very end, nothing to lose, no hope, no future... nothing, the end!

Kevin

Chapter 3 The beast

The once silent glen now dies. With the sound of crackling torches and muttering, Cooper still clawing at the metal pole. The first man that had shouted down the ravine, now stood in front of Cooper - a dark angry glare falls from the only visible bit of face that isn't hair. He lifts his flaming torch towards the figure and let's it brush against Cooper's arm, a loud tiger like snarl echoes through the glen and the face of the stranger begins to change. His front two incisors extend out of his mouth in a sharp, pointed manner. His eyes turn jet black covering all the white and colour and so deep they could scare the strongest of men. His skin stops being smooth and perfect - to red and irritated, and long white fingernails extend out the once normal hands.

The man moves forward in a way that states no fear of this creature; Cooper violently snaps at him with these new pointed teeth.

The man talks

"You see people, this is the face of your enemy, look no remorse or care. Now it was all show "

He takes his muddy shoe as he says this and plants it into Cooper's chest, pushing him further down the pointed pole

"Now Cooper you will pay!! Our daughters and sons shall be avenged, hiding among us as if you were our friend. Thought you could just move on to the next unexpected group? WRONG, we ken these glens better than anyone. To have sat at my table, MY TABLE, with my family, then you kill MY daughter "

He kicks a second time, this time with more passion. Blood splatters out Coopers mouth over the bearded man's leg. Four younger men start emerging from the woods carrying a large wooden box embellished in gold. It has long wooden braces that have been quite clearly hand carved to strengthen the box, it was built to last. No escape! What looks like homemade crucifixes, are also decorated onto the box. The figure now known as Cooper looks at the box and laughs out loud.

"Is that it the best you can muster, kill me and be done with it, you cloth wearing fools. "

He then bursts into a more evil laugh, and then starts to regain his strength. He begins pushing himself up the pole while continuing to laugh, as soon as he starts this, the kilted man next to him, immediately runs up and spears Coopers hand with a diamond topped spike, like the kind on the top of old English railings.

Cooper screamed into the night sky; birds flocked away from the scream. Then a second scream, as the man speared his other hand, then pulled the two arms together. Now the only way for Cooper to remove this would have to be destroy his hands. The now immobilised Cooper began laughing again. Metal wire is brought from a satchel lying beside the box. The kilted men begin slowly wrapping it round the spikes and pulling it together, then Coopers feet are spiked in the same manner and the same, hard looking bindings. Starting at the feet, criss-crossing upwards and then down from the wrists. Every turn of the metal confining him more and more, he looks around at his situation and realises

"I'm Fucked"

The kilted man looks down at the now trusted beast.

"Now you can't do anything, you like to feast on our young... well you're going to smell them for the rest of time "

Another kilted man starts carving a hole in the side of the box "eeeeeeehhhhhhaaaa youuu thiiink yooouu beeeat mee iiim forrrrrever"

Cooper spits out through his mouth along with blood

The men then stab their torches into the ground, and all converge on Cooper as he growls and spits at them, while he shouts out comments like "I'll fucking kill youuu!!!!", "you're Fucked !!!"   The kind of comments you say when you're angry at getting beaten and outsmarted! Especially when you have been getting away with something for so long.

They lift him up, carefully avoiding his face, only lifting him by the bindings, then lower him into the box. As he's placed in it, it becomes visible to him that his head has been placed on top of some kind of leather device? He twists his fang-based face left, then right and laughs a more fake laugh! This time into the sky. Two of the men lower large hooks into the box and grab the device under his head and lift it up then join it in front of Coopers face. A third man places a giant grey metal padlock on the front of it where there are two massive metal clips. Cooper is now thrashing about in a violent manner, the kilted men are applying leather bind, after leather bind, attaching it to pre-attached clips. After they are finished, he can't even move a muscle! All that is visible is his deep black eyes, staring directly at the bearded man. He stares back with no fear. All the other men are at the back of the waterfall digging and picking into the wall and soil. The water is pouring down on to their heads and body's. There now soaked kilts hang limply down their knee. They continue as if they haven't even noticed. The bearded man spits in Cooper's face

"You killed so many of us but, my daughter was everything to me you little bastard, you will feel pain for ever! We could tear you to bits, burn you or crush you but, I have no girl to love so you will spend all time in agony aware of existence always smelling passing blood but unable to act on it"

He spits on him again and grabs a giant wood lid, to match the wooden box. He places it on the end of the base and slowly starts sliding it forwards. As Coopers eyes stare, the last thing he sees is the dark sliding closer and closer, to his evil dark eyes and then gone!!

Sealed, the bearded man reaches for a hammer and starts hammering nails into the box, he moves in a succession around the box until he reaches the starting nail. He whistles loudly at the other kilted men, they stop digging and stare round, they then throw their picks and shovels down and move over. They all grab an edge of the box and lift, then they head over to the waterfall with it, as their boots splash into the stream. Destroying natures natural way, they all veer slightly back and push one end into the pre-dug hole. Then they all push and the box slides on wet and slippery mud. They keep pushing until the end is flat against the mud and the bearded man unwraps a blue and white Scottish flag from a leather pouch on the front of his kilt, to reveal what looks like black charcoal wax? He scribes the words "MORTEM" on the lid of the box.

Still visible they then start collecting rocks from the surrounding area and placing them in front of the box, until it's so covered not even natures going to move them, then the men all grab their flaming torches.

"It's done! No more will die from this beast"

The bearded man lowers his head as if praying

"Rip in peace EILIDH"

The men all move slowly back into the forest…………………………………..

Chapter 4 the hostel

Kevin sat to the back of the double decker Lothian bus, its pristine red and blue seats not even worthy of his three-day unwashed appearance. Kevin felt People were staring at him, a million bugs crawling all over him and stared at inanimate objects in anxiety. Just to pretend that people aren't staring - Kev feels isolated!

Suddenly this bus is enlarging, the driver no longer feels a few short steps away. Suddenly, there is miles between him and the front of the bus and the width is moving wider and wider apart...

There is an old woman turning around, taking and looking at him or.... is it just his imagination?

Thoughts are few and far between, Kev wonders if he's starting to die? Or having a heart attack? Or is this just panic?

His nose becomes blocked, his breath short. Should he get off?

Not far, only three more stops'!

Just hold on, pick an object outside and focus on that! Time has slowed, the bus seems to be taking forever, a million screams in his head. Damn two stops to go, Kev wobbles to his feet

trying to make it look like he is in control he presses the big red square button. Standing, staring into the distance - as if a normal person waiting on the bus stop arriving! More eyes on Kev, he shuffles down the isle of the bus, the driver looks at Kev with disgust. Possibly due to the fact he had counted his bus fair in Two pence coins. The driver pulls up to the stop and the doors his open.

Kev floats down the stairs.

"cheers pal " Kev blurts and walks off the bus.

The door closes as quickly as they opened!

Kevin moves away from the bus stop and shuffles in to the grassmarket towards an oyster and steak bar. He reaches into his inside pocket and pulls out a pair of sunglasses and puts them on. They are bright green, Kev had started wearing these when he was in his teenage years when he was smoking substantial amounts of green buds of weed! They had become like a second skin of vision for him, a comfort blanket.

as he came to the road and started to cross. A taxi flew passed his nose, almost touched it!

He ran quickly across and started heading towards a giant stone bridge, as he walks over the air hits him from the other side of the bridge.

A Cool wind, with thin bits of rain.

He had heard of the place he was headed, it's a place for a free meal and some shelter. Because he had been free loading with his aunt, until now he has never needed to use any of these places!

He approaches a bill board splattered in stick on advertisements, all in an array of squares and rectangles, so overlapped, that they look like an old wet newspaper, that had been plastered to an old board. A few more steps and then he sees it.

A church, a sanctuary, pushed back away from the rest of the Cow gate. One of Edinburgh's main nightclub strips, a dark dingy stretch of backstreet clubs and shitty wee pubs!

The door to church has three individuals outside one with tattoos of knifes protruding up from his neck to his ear, and a short curly haired little woman with bright red curly hair and a bomber

jacket, green in colour that looks like it had been used to wash shop windows for a week! Not to mention shitty black leggings, soaked in days of sweat and pish!

The other male is quite obviously the female's partner? Standing proud and tall as if waiting for his limo in the Chelsea area of London!

Covered in a large grey anorak with that horrible gritty texture. Also, wearing black out glasses even with the sides open on them and typical alcoholic black trousers!

Kevin approaches the door, as he gets towards it, all three of the characters aim the vision on him now. Although this is quite intimidating, he still doesn't feel half as nervous as on the bus!

As he looks at the door, there is a rusty sign saying

"24 TV RECORDING IN OPERATION" and a rusty old bell.

He goes to press it, the man with the knife tattoo places his hand firmly on Kev's shoulder

"am tam, wats your name chief? "

he says in a deep smoker's voice.

"Kev mate, wats up?"

"Well chief, I get called big tam that's ma handle. Ye ken if you need shit, I'm the one to see... how much ye paying for kit these days? "

"ten squid a bag mate, sometimes twelve" Kev says nervously

"Well boy, you need anything? You can get me a bell! ill dae ye it for eight squid a bag ma boy! "

He hands Kev a business card, as if they were exchanging gold bars, not injectable class A substance!

"Cheers man, will do "

Kev nods towards him and heads back towards the door. In his head he is thinking, ladies make up in an eight-pound bag! He sniggers.

In his head. He gets to the bell and rings it, the bell is loud and old fashioned. It takes a minute to ring and you hear footsteps approach and the door, creaks open.

An airy-fairy woman, quite thin with a squint in her eye, opens the door and looks at Kev

"come in " she says in a bored repeated voice

He shuffles through the door, as if all his dreams had come true!

The woman pulls him to one side as they pass the door, and looks him in the face

"are you on anything?"

"No" Kev replies,

"I've not touched anything in days " Kev relays.

"Good I hate people who are high ... I've been raped three times "

she says in to Kev's face.

While one eye looks at the ceiling and one at the floor.

The woman lets out a unstable shake and walks on, Indicating Kev to follow.

"ok then " Kev mutters quietly, making sure the psycho door girl doesn't hear.

He follows her down a stone passage and then reaches a large council style door ....

"You can sleep hear for one night only, just to get yourself together, then you're out! No drugs, nothing! If you are caught ill call the police and you will be lifted. I'll, make sure, of that ......

"I will bring you something to eat in about half an hour "

Kevin nods

"thank you "he says hopingly

The woman shuffles, of as if being pulled away by a rope, like one of those mimes you see with the black and white stripped jumper.

Kev moves in to the room, he has for the night. As he opens the door, things run through his head - like a Novatel room. White cotton towels and long bath robes, big king-size bed and all the trimmings. Free soap shampoo, flat screen tv and a little tea and coffee set just to finish of the almost perfect stay over!

 SMASH!! His dream explodes, in a cartoon style smash, as the door opens to reveal a complete concrete room. No paint, not even the floor. The only thing in the room, a small foldaway bed that looks like it hasn't been changed in years and a bed side unit with a jug of brownish water! A rusty white old school, fashioned radiator. The floors already have at least,

six visible bugs and all the corner's filled with mouse droppings. Kev sighs, and moves towards the folding bed. He lies down, and it creaks. Suddenly the floor becomes an option but, he sticks out the bed!

He closes his eyes and thinks about the journey there
....

Next thing, a hand is shaking Kev's shoulder

"are your awake son? here's something to eat "

It was the woman again, not a pretty sight to wake up to! He glances up to her shirt, it reads Theresa,

 It suited her, he sits round and excepts the steaming bowl of soup.

Every bite seems like the nectar of life, bearing in mind Kev hasn't eaten since he left his aunties! Theresa said,

"ye gain back out the night?"

"no, I've nae slept since Tuesday - I'm just going tae hit the sack " Kev said.

"Cool Hun, I'll just close the door over. You got a wee lock on the inside, a would lock it if a were you! night " she does another weird shake all over and then departs,

Leaving Kevin to his soup, he eats every bit and then waits a while for in case Theresa returns! Then reaches into pocket and peels out a squashed cigarette packet, puts

one in his mouth and lights it. He takes a long hard puff .... well that killed the whole of five minutes.

The 7th level of hell confirmed, Kev reaches in his back pocket

and pulls out a bag of smack, puts it in a golden tea spoon and takes a biro out of his other pocket. Places it in his mouth and inhales, the burning smack pours into his lungs, like a hot dream.

Waves of calmness pouring over him and all his troubles seem to pour away, nothing matters anymore!

Chapter 5 Darkness

Cooper stared into the abyss that they had made for him, little air not that he needed it, but it felt nice on his skin. No light, no noise, just the distant muffled noise of birds. Water and scents drifting into the pre-cut hole they had left to torture him with.

Escape? Is it a possibility? NO, his strength would only diminish in this casket. His power weaken. Unless, his luck was to change and fresh blood would happen to be coming down and pouring in, from that pre-cut hole? not likely!!! His eyes are moving around and around, the dizziness is so intense he moves In and out of conscious. He thinks back to a time where he fell from a large rock face about seventy years ago and he was without blood for two weeks. It felt like his body was on fire, and all he could do was think about it in agony, as he crawled to the nearest town.

This was now different, there was no hope of a small reprieve at the end. All there was, was blackness and the knowledge that over time he would go slowly insane forever. Not even death would save him. Without blood, petrification is his future! Slowly and painfully, until a living lump of stone occupies the large wooden box. He is now encompassed waves of colour, moving in and out of his mind. Sharp flashes of yellow, like lightning bolt shards criss-crossing, once where his eyes processed vision.

What must he do to survive this? his mind ponders, he thinks deep!

"Focus on memory" he mutters to himself.

His mind dips deep into his psyche, how far back shall he go and relive? He can't focus on anything, but the only thing Cooper fears - no more warm human blood!!

Now he counts back 54321…….

Suddenly, there is a face of a young girl BONNIE. She smiles back across a green back dropped field. The hills lifting into the sky, like the shape of broken glass. To her immediate left, she is met by a thatched house. Thick looms of dried hay and thatch, bounded together into an efficient, tight, water proof roof. Below an intricate mesh of perfectly slotted stones and peat, all linking into a little cottage.

The girl turns to meet the charming return of Cooper's seductive smile. He leans towards the girl and whispers in her ear

"Bonnie, I know the way this goes - you back off, I back on. You play hard to get, you still end up halving a walk with me tonight "

Bonnie turns her head into her shoulder and looks cutely towards him. Releasing her sexy smile, her long light brown curls resting just behind her shoulders. Her light coloured grey dress, long but revealing her skinny, light coloured skin, shoulders.

Cooper moves in a wee bit closer and blows gently on her neck. His ice-cold breath pinpoints on her soft warm neck, creating an instant reaction of cold meets hot. A thousand nerves activate on her body and Mexican wave down the girl in a quivering like motion. She whispers back

"Let's go then, honey "

He moves even closer and kisses her ear lobe so gently, his lips aren't even barley touching. A second wave of pure accelerated, exciting nerve - rushes through the innocent young girl.

The pair begin their walk towards the forest hand in hand.

They keep going deeper, as Cooper Is running his hand gently over her shoulder, she looks up at him. He is much taller, her deep brown eyes watched him with fascination . She knows he could be dangerous. This is only the second time she has met him and now's she's walking in to a dark wood with him but she doesn't care. Anybody that attractive could never hurt me, she thinks.

She skips round him and laughs excitably.

"Hey Cooper, if he finds out where we went... he'll kill, you ? "

She says in a non - caring way.

"Ha-ha yes, I suppose. I will just need to get you back in time for supper "

He says, smiling at the girl. Now just sending the exciting nerve reaction, with just a look. She is now his, he thinks!

 "I'm never staying here long, don't think of me as the local gal. I'm just finding ye interesting" she says.

While skipping forward.. Cooper looks in disgust at her chit chat and makes a mouth chatter gesture behind her back. He looks blankly at her, as she turns around and he drops his hand to his side his back and smiles politely.

"Yes dear, I've found you irresistible and unique from the second I laid eyes on you "

Cooper reply's in a seductive voice

She smiles back, in an easy bought manner. He smiled ahead again, the girl looked forward at him

- then unbuttoned two of her three buttons, upon the top of her dress neck line and pulled her top line open, to reveal her cleavage. Although Cooper was staring forward at this point, he could hear every pin prick, every increased heartbeat, every breath, he can hear it all.

He smiles, and whips round to Bonnie and slides up against her. Laying his lips against her soft red lips and gently kisses her without hesitation. She kisses back, in pure astonishment at the fast manoeuvre! He puts his hands gently around her shoulders and she puts her finger in between two buttons on his shirt and pulls him towards her, while walking backwards to the rock face. As her back gently cushions against the Stony grey surface, she lowered her hand to her skirt and hitched it up to her upper thighs to reveal frilly underwear White quartz in colour, then she slowly lowered them down and stepped out of them, while replacing her hand on her thigh with coopers. Once again, staring into those deep brown eyes, he kissed her again and moved in as tight as he could to her slim firm body!

She started to undo the large silver buckle on his waist, as he leaned in to kiss her neck. She lets out a sexually exited noise of relief and she felt very satisfied at this moment. But wait, she thought ……….

Something is different this time, other men she had been with, it had been good. Sometimes even great,

she had never felt this before, a cold pins and needles like feeling on her shoulder. Could this just be an intense sexual feeling? No, there's definitely something different. Now feeling a new sensation of wetness that is running on her shoulder, something is now very wrong.

She starts to shout out Coopers name, but what? Why? nothing happens but a shallow, gasp like, version of her previous voice. She looked down slowly in fear at her shoulder. What was once grey and pale skin coloured, is now a sea of splashed red against skin all blending in to every pore like sinking red paint on an orange peel . It's her own blood, with each breath pumping out down her body. Now frozen with fear, she turns to Cooper and looks in to his face. What was once his seductive blue calming eyes, now massive black pupils occupying his entire eyes. His skin arrayed with thin black capillary style veins, his mouth stretched and dripping, like wax down a candle . large teeth span his mouth like pointed polished nails. Fear has now immobilized her body, as she tries to shuffle away at the site of this ungod like creature!

 As fast as she tries, Cooper lifts the small girl by her hand about five inches high. Her small button white shoes dangling lightly above the ground, and for a second time Cooper plunges his now pointed jaws in to Bonnies arm. As she looks down in terror, she mutters in her new hollow voice

"Please don't kill me, I'm only eighteen, please! "

With this he sticks his finger in to her mouth and rips out her front tooth, a muffled scream of agony leaves Bonnie's mouth. Cooper laughs as he then snaps her wrist like a twig, she screams again and looks at him again with a look of mercy. He looks back at her and sighs

"But we are having such an enjoyable time"

He looks at her again ...

"ugggghh okay, that's fine, dinners over"

He moves her head up to a high height, a tear falls slowly from her beautiful brown eye as he snaps her neck. He drains what blood he can from her, and then throws her body aside like an old used newspaper. Then he uses a piece of her dress he had torn from her as a napkin to wipe his face.

Ahhh good times 5 4 3 2 1 ......

Back to darkness, this thought brought Cooper temporary clarity, it kept his mind together. He had found his lynch pin, he had killed tens of thousands of men, women and children. This would be enough to keep him sane for a long time, so many deaths to relive, so many exciting kills, this shall be my salvation in exile. Cooper shall survive, here we go again

12345... ahhh Jane

Flashes of colour pouring down like a melting rainbow, a thousand smarties - like clouds. All that ever mattered, no longer matters. Every time you get that feeling when you sleep in or lose important keys, gone. All that's left, is a drug fuelled bliss of stress free, pain free, worry free existence. What started out as that first cigarette as a kid to impress the girls, with tight Levi jeans, now transformed into a ladder of evil steps. One leading to another, nothing but misery increasing with each one. Only leaving an existence of dependence, instead of the innocence you started with. Trying to find that first freedom you had. Bang!

Kevs eyes burst open. what happening? But before he had even had a chance to form this thought, a skinny cold pair of hands wrapped round of his neck, fear floods through his body. The next thing he sees is a flash of a sharp knife, what was happening? Fear and shock ran through Kev's body, he feels a white light feeling in his head he struggles to focus his eyes and see what has happened. A tall skinny figure, with a shaved head holding Kev, half up off his bed. With a sharp, serrated edge hunting knife, tight up against his throat!

"Alright you little fuckin shit, give me all the kit, all the dough or I'll fucking cut you son"

The tall skinny man had a blue, faded dragon tattoo, right down his neck and a large scar under his eye. This coupled with a faded dirty denim jacket, just enough to complete the image of this evil junk infused thug. Kev was petrified, he didn't have the strength or the wit to fight off this maniac! He goes to reach in his pocket to give the man money, as he does the man runs the knife across the back off Kev's hand. The pain shoots to Kev's brain, like a cutting feeling, as if when you're trying to cut through a hard crust on bread. Then he bends Kev in to an arch and knees him in the face, things go white for a second. Two bright lights with criss-cross yellow lightning comes and goes in lines, away from them, the fuzzy image of the floor getting clearer! Clear now, he can see a tan coloured pair of Rockport boots. One plunges in to his stomach and then a shuffle in to his pockets and a feeling of things being pulled out of them. Another boot to the stomach and then the Rockport's moves away.

The door slowly closes, Kev gasps for breath, each breath getting easier and with a taste of blood. Why? He was thinking could this all have been some warped drugged up delusion? NO, it was real. The pain was real, the floor was real, what a shitty situation! The man rips his hand in to Kev's pocket, removing all the contents and then he moves on to the next pocket.

"Alright you wee dick, don't be back here again without paying me or with anybody else's smack, you little maggot"

 As he says maggot, the word becomes distorted, as he smashes Kev in the forehead with a knuckle duster.

Now, blackness, a non-thought sleep - just like anaesthetic, pain free, thought free, bliss. But, that can never last forever! Oh no, the first thing Kev feels is the bridge of his nose as he wakes up in a pool of his own blood In front of him. Then the pain from his hand, a massive sting unlike anything he had felt before. The shock must have shielded him from the pain, he tries to raise himself to his feet but fails. His body is just to dizzy, he lies there, just thinking about why his life had taken the path it did and thinks to himself is It even possible for it to have went another way? He tastes the blood in his mouth, a deep thick iron flavour, something that never agrees with the human taste buds. He pulls himself to his feet and slumps down on the bed and looks around the room in disbelief. Bang bang, another surge of pain from his hand. He searches his pockets on the off chance that the evil bastard has missed something, no such luck. He wipes the blood from his face and grabs a big chunk of bog roll for his hand and walks out the room. As he leaves, he looks back up the hallway. He sees the man sitting on a wooden chair, with the girl Theresa sitting on his lap smiling at him in a smug way.

He thought to himself,   LITTLE BITCH

The man smiled and blew him a kiss.

Kevin turned and walked out the doors, as he moved outside he was hit by darkness. Of this he was glad, as he was all sore and tired. The last thing he wanted was a large amount of peering tourists, or sun in his eyes!

He headed down towards the cowgate, a small scattering of cheap booze pubs and clubs. The lower side of Edinburgh's entertainment. As he walked, his injuries show. His hobbled steps, all muscular, trying to combine and repair. The pain has all but dulled, except the massive throb where Kev's hand was cut by the knife wielding maniac! Kev looked around to his left, a large picture of a hooded youth had been attached to the underside of the bridge. It towered the whole height as well, it was completely white with shades of grey. It was set in a way, where it would light up the entire bridge. Kevin, who still had a large amount of heroin running through his system, looked up and all the grey edges had a light vibration to them and a chemical shake. Kev had to look away, as this caused him an increasing panic feeling. Most likely a mix of the drugs and lack of sleep. He walked quickly away from the evil picture and out from with under the bridge, as he headed in to the cow gate he walked passed a bar named Faith! The sign metal and chrome finish, standing on the harling wall, like a rusted old shoe horn. As he walks, a Mercedes police vehicle approaches.

Fuck, fuck, fuck!!

Buzzing through his head, where would he tell them as residence? What if they knew he had been on smack? All the usual questions buzzed through his mind. He walked on, praying there was no comeback. Trying to glance in to windows to see behind him, just to give him a head start but nothing seems to come. They drive past peacefully and ignore him! Kevs breath is almost non-existent, forcing himself to breathe normally, is next to impossible! Tingling appears in his toes and fingers and a light fuzzy feeling in his head. He leans his hand on a fence to the left, on the outside of a big church and slows his breathing. He then heads back on his stroll, he checks his path ahead up and down. To his right, a window, all marble stone surrounding it. Kev smiles as he peers in the window, as he pauses a girl in a pink top is cutting a girls hair, she's wearing tight black leggings and Ugg styled boots. Her breasts were HUGE! Kev stopped to admire them for a second, she peers out at Kev in disgust. He moves on quickly, trying not to draw any attention to himself. Next thing, a huge spray of thick sticky water pours down his side

"Fucking smack head "

A small casual teenager and one other tall boy, stood smirking as he launched the contents of his can of juice down Kevs arm, Kev just looked forward but mumbled in rage!

" You fucking starting, you smelly bastard, I'll smash you, you wee radge "

The tall boy pulls the casual one away,

"Fucking ticket "

He shouts at Kevin as he is pulled away.

Kevin continues his way. A million scenarios running through his head, most of them where he is packed with muscle and stamps on the casual's neck. Or he is a dangerous gangster? That no one would mess with! Sadly, back to reality. None of this true. He is a miserable drug abuser that has nothing left, not even his last fix. He was headed to change that, well hopefully!

He carries on and keeps looking around, he reaches a kebab shop on the corner, he had been in that shop many times in his youth, pissed and collecting kebabs and pizza to end a good night. Many rungs back down the ladder, probably at one of the junctions where Kev could have decided to go either way - He glances in as he passes, it looks exactly the same as it did five years ago. The same wall paper, typical Turkish gig always stays the same. All good, it means you know what to expect. Further on to the right-hand side, again a pile of junkies and street filth sitting on a bench outside a metal panelled door. Kev knew about this place, a local hostel for the homeless. He now wishes he had gone there instead of the crazy place with the bald knife wielding psycho with the tattoo. He continues again and sees a crowd of girls, hockey players they all have small miniskirts on and knee-high socks. Kev immediately notices the crowd of legs and a rush passes through his body and shudders in his pelvis. He moves on down the street and the crowd begins to pass him, he stares at them all one by one, like he is a super model of life! They look back in disgust and most of them try and pretend they don't even see him, it hurts Kev as he knows the only chance he would have with girls like this is, date rape. The crowds pass and Kev is once again alone, on his way to human misery. Headed in the direction of his fix, he turns to cross the road and his vision directs towards a gleaming Tesco...

The windows bright shiny it might be his lack of sleep or drug infested system but the Tesco has become a visual field of cartoon, the interior an endless blanket of coloured packets, a floor of glistening crystal and every strip of lights intensifying it all. Kev falls in to the paradise and moves straight towards the gleaming drinks cabinet and reaches in for a glowing orange bottle, the words sprawl IRON BREW. Kev reached in to his sock and revealed a dirty pound coin and heads towards the checkout, suddenly everything becomes dry as if he had never had a drink in his life. The glowing bottle in his hand is the only cure for this evil curse, time has become scarce. He approaches the checkout and turns back to the golden shop .... gone! Nothing but dirty floors, desolate isles, rotten bread, every food a stomach-turning nightmare! The strip lights just burning his throat more, he knows if he takes a drink without buying it first the security guard with the large forehead will be down on him like a tun of bricks and he doesn't think he could take any more pain. He hands over his dirty one pound coin to the check-out assistant as the walls are creeping closer, he leaves swiftly. The guard with the large forehead stares at him with beady eyes, Kevin leaves the worn down dirty windowed Tesco, throws the orange lid open and pours it down his throat................

Snap goes the neck of an English minister, as Coopers hand fully extended, swipes away to the side. Reliving this memory was a great relief, his mind still locked in to an evil montage of mayhem and fear of tortured souls. Suddenly then something has changed .... movement but what? Coopers mid dream evaporates in a flash of light and suddenly he was back in the box. There was something in here but How? Were they releasing him? Has someone else found him? Who cares? His eyes force downward towards the movement to see what it is? Next a small squeak.

"It's a RAT! Cooper, excitably, thinks his salvation was finally here. He moved his eyes down to the small furry beast but how could he see it? When he's buried under a waterfall, how can there be light? Then it catches his eye, the hole the bearded men had made to torture him with smell and sound was exceptionally bigger! They had messed up, he could get free and crawl out this gap. YES, he thinks.

First lunge down to free your hand, and grab the rat, then drain its blood, then use that power to wriggle free and finally, use the strength in your leg to widen the opening!

At last - freedom from this hell! Right, let's go but wait... nothing happened. His arm didn't move but why? He tries to move his fingers but they are completely solid like rock as are his toes. He can now notice by wriggling, that his entire lower arms and lower legs are completely stone. Unmovable, there goes that plan. How long had he been in deep thought? For his body to reach this level of petrification it must have been a long time. The last time this happened he had no blood for two weeks and a spot the size of a fly, was all that appeared on his entire body! All he now had was thought, he put is brain in to deep maths mode and he calculated... No, he must be wrong. Had it really been that long? Two Hundred and Fifty years, or there about. Had time really have bended that much into his mind? He will be in here forever he thinks in despair, NO he can't let this happen, must keep faith. I will be freed one day – OK what's next? Something else?

Close to another similar incident where he had escaped and prevailed.

"THE GREAT WHITE CHURCH"

Chapter 8 the blue bed

Standing outside Tesco leaning on a wall Kev feels the instant relief of the cold juice pouring down his gullet, waterfalls of relief. Slide down his neck, every single inch of moisture pouring down until reaching his stomach. Creating one final explosion of exciting sugar rush and relief, for one minute all is problems disappeared in to one reliving second. These moments never last long, the pain has left. The Tesco has returned to normal. He looks across the road, a large block of flats towering into the sky, he only looks for a second before the sky becomes a painful to his eyes. Black rims closing in from the sides of each eye every second he continues to look. The sky isn't just white as it should be, millions of multi coloured worms wriggling all about filling his entire field of vision, like looking through a kaleidoscope but much more drug induced. He slowly he starts to walk every step becoming harder, time was against Kev now he had to make it to Davie's and get some sort of relief, or bad things would start to happen no hope! No past! Nothing!

It was - all about reaching the flat, that was all that mattered. He just hoped he would be welcomed at Davie's. He was like family but his girlfriend was a complete and total little bitch and she hated Kevin! And unless Kevin was brandishing a briefcase of solid gold (which he wasn't) then he would be an unwelcome guest and deemed nothing but a sponger in her eyes. All he wanted was a chance to change. He couldn't fail this time, or it was all over for real this time. He walks into the entry for the scheme, tall concrete pillars on each side, a long winding road untouched by maintenance, potholes broken kerbs rubbish blowing back and forth in a mini cyclone of trash. He walks past the entrance to the large, overpowering flats and heads through a black gate this leads him upwards alongside an unpainted tall metal fence, the more he climbs the higher the drop behind the fence gets and eventually Kev is looking down to the car park of the scary tall flats. As quick as the road rises it now descends just like a giant backbone, a pointless rise completely unnecessary he thinks, why had they not just carved the road all at the same.

 Kev feels a blinding, white pulse in his vision then two yellow tunnels appear, his legs no longer seemed attached hanging jellified from his body. His chest turns tight, there appears a tight pressure in his stomach like a water balloon, he pulls his body up against the unpainted fence, like a wave as he toils to hold it together. An Asian woman who is sitting on the kerb with her younger daughter stands up and walks away, as if he was a zombie edging towards them coming closer to eat her brains. People fear the wasted and drunk more than the normal man, because the rules are out the window, common decency and respect are gone and not even the intoxicated individual is sure what he is capable off. He gets his vision back and the tremor passes, he peers ahead to see a dusty blurred out phone box and looks to his right, then up to empty flat he had been in previously, partying. Full of complete skanks and sluts, memories of snorting Cocaine off a flat stomach and taking tequila with lemon and salt. The memory flashed into his mind like a taunt as he now knew that no girls would even look at him now. He had reached the end of the party, life youth all gone only addiction left. Then his eyes veer to the left to reveal a blacked out convenience shop, no windows just a metal mesh door, poorly painted exterior walls and a Sign for cheap cider outside. This was no shop, this was a prison cell that sells food, alcohol and newspapers.

"Stop getting distracted"

 he thinks.

He now focuses forward and paces faster, as he sees the staircase leading up to Davie's. The length looks ridiculous a long grey stretch of steps, he searches back, in his cloudy memory, had they always been this high or was he just crashing badly? Suddenly he feels a thousand eyes on his back the pain in his stomach returns, along with the feeling that something is about to go terribly wrong. He races towards the stairs and looks up them, the image of one of those funny black and white pictures where staircases turn upside down and backwards, appears in his mind and overtakes his real vision. He still carries on anyway, then he looks down and sees a fresh cigarette packet, suddenly all other thing halt, he stops looks around and reaches down to check it, as always, its empty and disappointing. He turns the corner into a doorway with a giant metal door, barley glass in' it more of a Smokey dusty Perspex glass. He hits a two and then a one and presses call, an Evil inverted ring pulses through kevs ears he presses again almost instant it makes a loud delayed beep, and a voice slurs out the metal buzzer.

"yea who is it "

The voice slurs

"it's Kev mate ".

He reply's

The door releases with a long constant beep as it does, Kev grabs the door and pulls it open he shuffles in. He enters in to the stair immediately met by a damp smell of human urine, concealed with garbage and poor attempts at bleaching, he attempts to hold his breath as in the past he had become a custom to this with the frequent visits to buy heroin, from Davie. He pulls up the stairs and reaches the number twenty one door, almost instant it whips open and Kevin is met by Davie. He is short but well-built, square shoulders and a square haircut to match. He's wearing a nice leather jacket tattered by time but in a nice way to make it look antique styled, he grabs kevs hand and pulls him in to give a pat on the Shoulder.

"alright chief you look like shit mate, needing a wee break matey come in "

He says in a very inviting way

Kev sighs in relief and nods at him, he almost starts to cry but contains it and enters. Kev walks in to the living room a long room, with very low ceiling and an odd coloured blue carpet, he sees a woven basket chair with a white cushioned interior he falls in to it, and a wave off calmness sweeps over him. He feels the numb head you feel after a long bout of anxiety. Davie throws him a cigarette out of a golden Benson and hedges packet and a lighter, Kev immediately flips the poison infested stick in to his mouth and lights it, it just amplifies his calm and he looks up to Davie.

"what's the chances of getting put up for a couple of days mate? "

kevs asks desperately to Davy

Davy looks uncertain

As he well knows, keeping business and pleasure separate is essential. He picks up a bong pipe and burns a metal gauze while sucking in the smoke, it fills up like a burning building but with creamy white smoke. It looks like you could even take a bite out of it just like double cream. He fills the bong and like a backdraft implosion , he let's go of a hole at the neck of the pipe and the smoke swooshes out in seconds, Davie closes his eyes and lets out a few short airless coughs and then blows out the smoke in a stylish blast of white vast vapour.

"see the thing is kevs, if bonnie knows I got any cunt staying here, she will panic the social will cut the housing benefit. You know, there is too many big nosed fucking snitching cunts about you ken ... but she's up in inverness doing her course and she's away till Tuesday I can help you out till then chief "

Davie says trying not to look Kevin in the eyes, instead looking uncomfortably staring at the floor.

A look of relief fall's on to kevs face, that was three days, it's pathetic to think that when you get that bad that three days can seem a great thing but that meant a starting point.

Would it go bad? Who knows?

It meant he could finally get some sleep safely without knife wielding junkies robbing him and plunging him deeper in to this rut he was already in. Kevin and Davie chat for a few hours while he explains the evil times that lead him to be there Davy throws in the occasional comment like

" aww man that's fuckin brutal "

 or

" fuckin ticket, we will find that Robbing baldy bastard, what a fuckin melon and uncle Davie will show him exactly who's boss "

He says this and slides his hand in to a gold and silver knuckle duster while making punching motions in mid-air. It was time to leave kevs knew although Davie trying to help he was getting more wasted by the second and more ridiculous too, and the last thing Kev needed was more drugs or booze

Kev stands up and shakes Davies hand

" mate I need to get some sleep buddy I'm going to hit the sack for a bit "

Davies nods and hands him a pre-rolled joint and two cigarettes

" cool matey get yourself together and we can sort you out from there use the spare bedroom there's a single bed in there chief "

Davy says while his eyes can barely even focus

 " cheers pal ".

Kev replies.

He turns towards the room while clutching the cigarettes, as if some crazy bald bastard is going to take them away from him. He heads into the room the same blue carpet all the way from the living room, peeling through the hall into the spare room. As he enters the first thing he sees Is the single bed with similar blue covers, the look old and unused, as if they were a prop made to resemble a forgotten room. He slips his jeans down and throws his top off, he rips the covers back and climbs in to the coldness of the sheet, it creeps up his legs a and spreads across his back its quite a relief , he reaches across and puts the joint in his mouth and lights it. A long hard draw brings him further in to relief, as the creamy wet smoke slides in to his lungs a wave of cool spreads his chest, with a tingle of pins and needles he releases the draw, and a cloud of thin white smoke engulfs the ceiling dissipating slowly in to nowhere but beyond the human visual spectrum. He dabs the spiff in to a green glass ashtray he lays back and closes his eyes. The images of sharp forestry trees in neon blue are zig zagging across his blank eye canvas, he fantasises about white pigs and golden river's across bridges, and then a girl almost fabricated from nowhere. Most sexual fantasy's in the brain exist from reality, this girl a complete drug, alcohol, weed and lack of sleep-fiction. He is thinking of pinning her strongly against a wall as she bites her lip in excitement, then she takes his hand and runs it up her inside leg until reaching soft lips covered with lace panties, as the pair of young lovers are intertwined they breathe closely in to each other's breath words exchange in ears ….. but back in reality Kev has reached in to his boxers, expecting a large erect penis to wank off, but Instead due to all the alcohol and drugs he is to find a shrunken bloodless, limp, poor excuse for male anatomy. He gives up all hope of anything happening sexual real or fictional. He was probably unable to properly urinate never mind cum. He takes his hand back out of and sighs, the image in his head of the sexy girl smashes like a bull in a china shop and returns to the jagged trees. Then no trees, then darkness, tomorrow would be different he thinks. Fresh start, new hopes then oblivion no thought, no vision just nothing ....

Good Night Kevin!

Chapter 9 Daddy and daughter time

Jimmy was a man of simple things, good food, family, warmth in his home, a gentle man. All things considered by any human standard a good man. He did what was right but never forced issues or started fights, a submissive man. He looks up to his daughter Katie who has now became taller than him at the age of just seventeen, she smiles back at him she loves her dad and he loves her. They head towards the treeline now hand in hand they enter the wood.

"dad what we going to get for supper?"

Katie says down to her father

"well lass there's two clean options and all that I want on ma table the night is a big fat bird or a long tasty fish or two"

The pair continue, nattering about their tea, away into the wood. They come to a clearing there is a medium sized stream winding its way through like a vein pulsing on someone's arm. The clearing, as quick as it starts, continues disappearing into a triangular flow like manner into the distance. The father hands Katie a long bit of thread like weaved rope, and almost instantly she knows what to do with it. And She leaps to a centre stone and skips over to the other side of the stream, and clips the rope to one side of a tree bark. Then gently launched the rope back to her dad, he repeats the process linking a home fashioned hook into soft tree bark. He then pings the line, it makes a light vibrating noise, he then proceeds to lower five hanging hooks at different size from the line. Each one hangs into the stream ,the father then stands back to admire his work, then looks around to his daughter, she looks back in acceptance and they both reconvene on the same side of the river they chat for a while. Then her father's eyes focus sharp on something,

A BIRD.

A pheasant, beautiful in colour, its feathers extending from him, like glorious wrapped dollar bills. The creature had wandered in by foot, bobbing along in a mathematical precise steps. Stopped now with the concept of food at its beak, the creature stops to dine on a glorious section of shrubs. The father pushes Katie behind him, hushing her, then reveals a blowpipe. They both lower down to half size and creep slowly forward, they reach the edge of the stream and stop.

"we don't want to spook it Katie slowly but surely"

She nods back at her father then he moves, the blowpipe to his lips and inhales wait …..wait ……andddd. Suddenly the previous fixed, fishing line jangles and Katie and her dad immediately whip round, the bird shoots of at twenty miles per hour away. The ground dissolves underneath katies father plunging him sideways in to the stream, an swell of side way water is launched from the stream, all over Katie s legs. After the aftermath of the whole situation ends, they both look round at each other and burst in to laughter. Although dinner was lost, it was fine, a father and daughters' bond still brought humour to the situation. He looks back round at the fishing line and one of the dangling lines was still twitching like a tight guitar string, he smiles again.

"Look girl, I'm wet anyway I'll go down and see what we got"

Katie nods

"ok father I will nip back to the house and get cloths to dry you"

He smiles

"ok my dear"

Katie stands up and shakes herself down. Her father, from head to toe, is wet and covered in mud, slime, moss, and everything else a stream can provide. Katie is walking away, and Jimmy has his back turned.

swwwwiiishhh

 There is a fast like wind noise and then a recoil of wind and leaves moving without accord. He turns to try and find her, to see his beloved daughter gone.

Hmmmm

 Had she made it out of the forest? Impossible, where is she he wonders, he peers around to find her.

 Oh, there she is, how did she get so far away? Wait, there is someone with her. Fear grips her father, suddenly all the reports of a killer in town flip in to his mind, he rubs the water from his eyes and focuses on the situation. As he is about to shout, his beloved daughters name, he then suddenly witnesses the worst thing a father could. The figures alongside his daughter is a MONSTER. He sinks his teeth in to her neck and drains the life from her in front of him. He is about to scream in terror, but as the figure kills his daughter, he cries into his arm, as the beast peers around the vista scouring for more prey! He then lowers himself deeper in to the stream to avoid this creature finding him and then must watch in horror, as the abomination tears his beautiful little girl to pieces, unveiling every nightmare he has ever conceived. After dismembering and scattering his daughter like she meant nothing, her father's eyes felt the despair leave and be replaced with anger, fury, burning RAGE!

Revealing himself to this monster would be pointless, he could now see him, COOPER.

His mind explodes in anger, after all the village had done for this wolf among the sheep, all that was left now was revenge!

He sat biding his time, waiting impatiently. NOW the beast was gone, exiting the forest unaware to the fact that he had been made. It was revenge time, this creature un-pure and godless must pay for his sins.

This "VAMPIRE" a taker of things, a parasite from the shadows. No morals, no remorse, a creature that could never be an equal only ever a taker of all things good. Immediately it threw out all common myths he had heard about these creatures. Sunlight was obviously not a problem like in legend. Cooper had been seen with people countless times during the day.

Crosses? He had been at church several times praying for his own victims so that leaves fire, stakes in the heart, and garlic but what one to use ………

FIRE ………… yes, that shall be this monster's demise after what he's done to my Katie. He lifts his hands from the stream in a fist motion and slams them into the edge of the bank of the stream. He forces his body upwards. He tears out of the stream with anger but also determination, his feet follow and then his body springs to the edge of the stream, all that once was has now past, there shall be no more mister nice guy, no more father, no more hero! He walks in a broken manor towards the opposite side of the forest that Cooper had left.

Heading towards town centre he approaches a large wooden door, enriched with fine carvings and green varnish, not just any door, a true work of art. His mud-covered hand slams against the perfect door sending splats off in different directions hitting all the surrounding stone. No answer, he slams again like an enraged beast.

The door begins to unlatch from behind and then slowly opens, a terrified old man with glasses and white hair, in what looks like a woman's striped gown peers round the crack

"what is it is every thhiiinngg ookkk..."

He stutters, the father pushes his way in while making a hush gesture with his finger, they both huddle in to the small wooden cottage and convene in the living area.

"what is it"

the frightened bed shaken man asks, as looking at his mud-covered friend.

he reply's in a determined voice

"we have a monster in our midst Daniel" he says

"a monster"

 Daniel says confused

"what kind of monster are you okay?"

He repeats

Normally this kind of statement would cause concern and instant disbelief of the truth, but Daniel knew his friend, and knew that he was not a drinker or the kind of man to just invent complete nonsense.

He looks down to his feet and tears fall like a precision rain drops, and disappears into the flooring groves.

"an unnatural beast of the worst kind, a hideous beast COOPER!!

It killed.... It killed .... IT KILLED MY KATIE"

The grief overwhelms him and tears just now stream down his face, Daniel steps forward and puts his thin hand on to his friend's shoulder and calms him. As the tears slow, the look of anger comes back Daniel peers at him knowing that the anger was there.

"Right, we need to contact Zee"

Zee was the man of authority in the village

"NO" he replies quickly,

"This will need to be dealt with, with care. If this creature gets to use his cunning ways, He will win. We needs a small group. This monster has been living among us for months and tricking us, playing family and freeloading."

"WE EVEN GAVE THAT BASTARD A HOME... We will need your expertise in traps, all the things you have made for me to feed the village, are just what we might need to save it"

He looks at him now with an evil look of pre knowledge of what's coming, a perfectly formulated plan! The kind of thing only careful planning could work. It had to work, this creature could not continue!

Cooper

Kevin wakes, before his eyes have opened a thousand birds scream in his mind as the gentle chirp of a single bird is outside. He wriggles his fingers to see if they can still move, by the pain in his head there was every possible chance he had suffered a stroke during the night and was completely paralyzed. He was lucky and probably over paranoid from all the drugs he could move. He dared to open an eye, light drips in stinging every step of the way, ok that wasn't the worst he thinks, now the other eye ok here we go full vision, full movement in my fingers we got something here. His eyes begin to focus on the ceiling ripple effect, aertex adorns the ceiling, and a giant paper planet shaped shade hangs lightly moving left and right with passing breeze. He scowls around to fully take in his environment, the walls couldn't be further from the colour of the sheets. Terracotta orange, badly painted in every way, just forced on by under skilled home makers, in the hope of matching their local Littlewoods catalogue. He reaches out the bed and lifts a cigarette in to his mouth and lights it, the wave of calmness rushes through Kevin's body, almost making him want to reverse his waking process and drift back to sleep,

BUT NO.

He must change, he must help himself all must be different today. He float's up almost without touching the covers, they fall to the floor. He looks at his clothes piled onto the floor, there is almost a cloud of vapour rising from them. no this would not do, how can he get a job, get a future with this set up. He looks down at his boxers, a large Scotland flag echoes through a pile of urine, dirt and food stains. Not right he thinks, on to a change! Kev walks out the room and peeks his head out into the hall, stuff scattered all along it like a car boot sale stretched out. He creeps out and his eyes catch a cupboard door slightly ajar, he slides his skinny fingers round it and pulls the door open a bit further, there are six Samsung, thirty two inch televisions, boxed, sitting in a neat stack, like neatly packed dominoes. He took a minute to calculate the value in his head then sighed, as he knew he would never see that kind of cash soon. He continued down the hall and then reached another door ajar, this time he poked his head in the door and looked. He focused through in darkness, there was a large double mattress lying in the middle of the room neatly lined up against the wall. Davy is propped up on several pillows wearing giant black female Primark style sun glasses, and a large fluffy hat with hanging fluffy dog ears. Kev makes a hissy zip noise with his lips and Davy grumbles and looks up.

"oh, right bud I'm going to get some shifts can I borrow some gear "

Kevin whispers gently

Davy looks blankly at him like it's the first time they have met, then as the cogs and wheels crush out the drugs and alcohol, he continues to glare then it all comes rushing back. Oh, yea he has Kevin in his house, his brain formulates a plan for Kevin with basic instinct. He points towards a chest of drawers and turns underneath his covers and pulls them over his head.

"Cheers mate ".

Kevin moves towards the drawers.

He pulls out a pair of white Nike socks and a pair of tartan boxers, then a pair of black jeans and a blue and brown shirt. He's about to walk away then he reaches back and grabs a white tee-shirt and heads back to his room. He is walking along the hall when he spies a hairdryer, he grabs it and heads in the room and dumps it all on the bed. He grabs his mud coated shoes and heads back out this time heading the opposite way and moving in to the bathroom. He looks round quickly, now a momentum has taken over him, self-depression was now gone. He looks at his options, a nice white towel hanging, a full bottle of lynx Africa and a yellow and white bic razor still unused. He grabs the bundle and hops in the shower, he has his shoes with him and throws them to the back of the shower. He pulls a cord hanging from the ceiling and without even having to play with the shower controls it bursts into life, the pressure isn't too great,

"but hey"

he thinks, it's clean running water, more than he has seen in days. He slips under in an almost afraid manner, but then the water provides the best relief in the world. His chest becomes warm and safe and a pressure lifts off his entire body. He stands for just a few moments and enjoys the love of the water. He then fills his greasy hair full of the lynx and spreads it around his entire body the whole shower fills with the scent in a vapour like manner. He looks down at his feet horrified to see black water running off his body, slime that should be running off a coal worker not a young man like Kevin. He chooses to ignore it and continue using the lynx, he then reached for the razor he smashed a handful of the lynx on to his cheeks and started pulling the razer down his shameful beard and began rinsing .The shower stops and the steam clears and out emerges a new version of Kevin, clean shaven and smelling fine. He thought, how I could have felt so bad, so destroyed and not realise it.

He sat down on the toilet and put his last cigarette in his mouth and lit it. While sitting enjoying the slow puffs in a steam sealed room he puts his head back and gives his mind one final clear. Once done he slipped on the new boxer shorts, followed by the white tee-shirt. He buttoned up the new black jeans and pulled on the socks with wet resistance. He then looked round to his new cleaned shoes and grabbed them and headed to his make shift room. He immediately plugs in the hair dryer and places it in his shoe like a mechanical ankle, and then leaves it screaming away as the shoe gently steams. Now he buttons up his shirt and

WOW

 Ready to go he thinks he finishes dressing and he heads back down the hall towards the front door. On the way out, he notices a small pile of pound coins he grabs four and continues. He walks down the stair and on approaching the metal exit door, he pushes a stainless steel button labelled push for exit, a large whining beep fills the stair behind him. He then pushes more, and the light explodes in to his eyes like a flash bang grenade. It takes about ten seconds for his eyes to adjust then back to his nightmare, the day before. All with a different outlook on life the sky seemed different, while still being grey it now had a much calmer feel . Yes he could do this he thinks, what a day to repair his life surely anybody with this attitude should get a fair chance, it must be the case that only the people who don't care about change are the ones who would never get help or a break.

 IF ONLY LIFE WAS LIKE THAT

 he sniggers internally in his brain

He heads back down the road, past the railings, then a shudder hits him as he sees Tesco looming over the verge. He looked again just to feed the fear in his brain one last time. Then started heading up another way towards the road bypassing it all altogether. Bad memories that stick he thought! Now he makes it to the main road. Although he has cleared his head with a bit of sleep and repair, nothing can hit harder than addiction and human misery. Suddenly a wave of pain enters his abdomen and he cringes for a second in to the centre of his body and he feels it all in one fast burst of memory, the relief from past times of burning his pain and anguish with heroin. His mind flashes to a teaspoon in his hand and a lighter burning under it creating a sludge, like burned treacle in the spoon a sharp needle moving slowly towards the spoon. The vision towards the spoon explodes, then SNAP the vision vanishes Kev shakes his head in a frenzy rage and slaps his own cheek.

"No this is not happening again today. I just got myself fuckin sorted. Not today this is the day for change! "

He says this loud enough for a young student, walking past, to pull a few steps away from him. She feels the need to put distance between her and the obviously, contaminated with drugs. He doesn't even notice her, he continues up the road until reaching a crossroads. On his left a row of shops, built under a canopy made of polished stone, soaked in the constant rain that plagues this city. He runs over having no regard for the traffic, the cars take little notice of him, they just veer round him while shaking their heads at him. He looks in each shop window hoping for job vacancy…

Nothing not even one, he sighs and moves on but what's this in the corner of young Kevin's eyes?

A NOTICE!

 wow that's perfect, a pub, he scampers over in excitement. Oh yes this is it he thinks when he sees the word

 "wanted"

 a new job, new house, meet the right girl at the bar, finally get clean and put this whole life behind him and start a fresh. He looks down into a grey, Austin martins wing mirror and sorts his hair, still under the long term influence of heroin and cannabis, he doesn't even realise there's a driver in that Austin martin, the driver looks at him in disgust. Kevin takes a deep breath and pushes into the bar. On entering, his eyes are aimed downwards, in nervous fear. When you focus like this away from reality, whatever you focus on starts to becomes a new reality!

So, the floor was the focus of this insecurity, he stares hard suddenly the floor was no longer a mass of brown, but an intricate criss-cross of wooden slats blessed with shiny, polished finish of varnish. People walk past such things every day, their brains trained to ignore it, the time, the effort that somebody has to put into it. Normal people are too busy for that. The only people with that kind of time are closely scrutinized by a shaking junkie. He moves in closer. The first thing that draws his attention, a giant stags head adorning the wall, the back wall. overpowering the bar like a god judging and protecting everyone under its cover.

He looks his head up to the left, he is met by an amber display of glory, a wall of fine Scottish whiskeys and spirits all lit by beaming lights and reflecting off each other, creating the impressive array of an amber door way. A well-dressed barman with a neat well-trimmed beard and a woven green jumper, stands in front of the amber doorway. His hair perfect, spiked as if each strand of hair had been gelled, individually into perfect little peaks. So, you can imagine how insecure the perfect barman was making Kevin feel. He leaned on to the edge of the perfect pine coloured bar, his hand reflecting at him in the perfect high shine varnish. The barman alongside a loyal patron both take notice of Kevin as soon as he moves towards the bar. No matter how hard he was trying to blend in he was always going to look an outsider, you cannot bury all those months of abuse under one outfit and night's sleep. The barman moves a step closer.

"what you having pal "

The bar man pushes towards Kevin.

"Ahhh nothing mate, I'm here about the ad in the window I'm looking for some work"

The barman looks at the patron and then looks uncomfortable, he shuffles for a second.

"hmm yes, I think the brewery might have someone, what experience do you have buddy "

He said in a pleasant polite manner trying to treat Kevin with the same respect he would show anyone.

"I haven't had any experience in bars but I'm a hard worker and I'm good at getting here on time "

Kevin pleads

The bar man looks unconvinced, as he sends this look Kevin's way, he looks at the barman then the patron, and the paranoia sets in.

THEY WERE LAUGHTHING AT HIM!!

 Kevin feels a sudden rush of anger, all the drugs running out his system stretch out in his blood supply, his body tightens each pulse of his veins and his heart running faster. He sat there feeling his eyes pulse as the barman went to speak.

"yes pal I will be honest with you we really are looking for someone with a lot of experience to run the bar on my off shifts thanks for coming in and good luck "

He says in a final phrase

Kevin's growing rage ignites in to a vile wash of disappointment, disgust he closes his eyes for a second and lets the pulsing feeling spread. The pulses spread and become more body wide, he opens his eyes and all his vision has now a tint of red, the rage had now consumed him, and he could no longer contain it!

"for fuck sake mate I'm trying my best here and you're not even willing to give me a chance you're a dick standing there all perfect you don't even know how important this is to me "

The bar man, and patron look at each other

"look buddy it's not personal it's just the rules of employment we have, now please leave I'm asking you nicely "

The patron stands up, Kevin looks both of them up and down, turns to walk out, he slams a coat rack against the wall and storms out the last thing he hears is .

"fuckin junkie"

He bursts out into the busy world people bustling up and down taking no notice of him, there was no point in remaining here, he moved onwards and upwards. He then went in to a fudge shop and four more bars and a corner shop all with the same dismissive attitude. He was about to lose hope until he reached a food shop, he almost walked past the wanted sign he swept back and looked at it.,

MALE/FEMALE WORKER REQUIRED TO DELIVER

BAKED POTATO PRODUCTS TO LOCAL OFFICES

COLLECT PAYMENT AND RETURN CHANGE

 MUST BE REALIBLE AND TRUSTWORTHY ….

Oh my god he could do that, anyone could do that!

 it was his job, it had to be, he looked in the window and summed up the manager, a gentle looking man he must be easy to chat to. The fears were completely gone now and confidence was as its high, well high as it could be. He pushed and opened the door, a small bell chimes above him. As it did he approaches the red painted desk, on approach the man turned and looked at him as if he was a customer

"how can I help young man? "

He says while picking up an empty polystyrene container, Kevin looks at the container in disgust and says with his new-found confidence.

"my pal I'm here for the job I'm your man this job was made for me, I'm the cork in your champagne "

The man stares at him for a second, shocked at the speed this sentence has left Kevin's mouth. Still amazed at the fact that this scrawny little junkie isn't wanting a baked potato and instead is wanting to work in his family business. The old man's brain racks for a fast response, Kevin begins to look uneasy, the confident smile and eyebrow lift descending into confusion. The man looks at him and states

"sorry lad but you're not quite what we're looking for here"

The look that had now changed, it started from joy, to uncertainty, now it sunk deep in to the lower levels of hell. Sweat forms on his head and his vision becomes skewed red again, aimed directly on the man everything goes white …………………..

about fifteen minutes later.

Two well-built police officers drag the rage fuelled wriggling and writhing Kevin backwards out the takeaway door, followed by the shop worker screaming Brazilian words at him that were quite clearly not pleasant!

The police were fighting every inch of their strength to contain the small framed Kevin. They are approaching there white Mercedes police car that had been abandoned in the middle of the road, causing absolute traffic chaos, while an array of spectators had amassed. A secondary police van whips up and two further officers exit. One officer moves towards Kevin and the other opens the back doors to reveal an aluminium cage, they drag Kevin as he is foaming at the mouth in rage and launch him in with the combined effort of three large men. Almost instantly the fourth officer slams the inner cage door shut, Kevin thrashes around inside the metal box like a hammer head shark out of water. They slam the exterior doors closed and all goes silent for them. Kevin calms down now realising it was the end of his rampage and there was no point in continuing.

He could hear the shop owner giving angry statements to the police, alongside passers-by's, siding with the poor shop owner man.

 if only they had known who the real victim was, he thought, he knew he was fucked, this wasn't going to go well. No not well at all so much for his day of new starts ………………

Jimmy a Daniel are in the church for nearly twenty-four hours batting and hammering, one of them keeping a close eye on the street for any signs of Cooper. but he was home relaxing after of a feast of poor jimmy's daughter. The only thing keeping jimmy going was the revenge of his daughter,

It was all he had left, the only thing that had stopped him committing suicide. eventually as Daniel swept a tired forehead of sweat away, they were done, They looked at each other in accomplishment

"This will work"

"he must have no idea, or we will be finished"

Jimmy states

"Yea I think it's the one Jimmy, all angles have been covered"

Daniel replies

All that was left was to snare him, That seemed easy but jimmy was thinking one wrong mistake and he could kill them all in a flash with the speed he had witnessed. There would be no hope for any of them, they have one final check then move out the doors to the village.

Cooper rises to the sun beating in the window, the taste of blood still fresh in his throat, but all most instantly sending craving through his entire body for more. He had learned to suppress this, his evil body would let him feed every hour if he let it, but that was too dangerous that would draw too much attention and would result in him eventually being caught. He had to be careful. These creatures he shared life with, were Neanderthals, simple and superstitious, but not the kind of mob violence you want to encourage.

He sits up in a rapid flash of blur. he whips over to the stone sink and straightens his hair into place with ease and wipes down his outfit and checks his body over for blood off his latest victim. There was none and he very rarely needed to wash his clothes as he didn't sweat, so you would be amazed how clean things can be kept when you take that out the equation. He was all set to go, another day of blending in with these overgrown apes, living with these simple village idiots, that was the way of things. They were too stupid to ever click on or to ever catch him.

WHAT FOOLS HA

The thing about folklore and fable of his kind, was always sunlight, all people that seeked to destroy or locate his kind in the past, they claimed on the fact that sunlight harms creatures like cooper, and burns them to an ash. This was simply not the case sunlight has no effect on Cooper whatsoever, apart from the fact he cannot develop any kind of tan his skin, he remains pale like a daisy first opening on a meadow in spring. So, he thought as these village people were searching for a self-igniting person. he was in the clear and free from threat. All he had to do was keep playing Mr nice guy and it was all good. He opened his door took a step out, his face warmed by sunshine and the glare of a thousand beams pouring through the trees. As it hits his cold, chalk like face, an almost sandstone look engulfs his skin. He yawns and stretches out.

What a day yesterday was, he thinks back and smiles,

suddenly a woman runs across his field of vision holding a large wooden box, followed by another man in green tartan robes. He thinks to himself, strange, but moves in closer to inspect as he walks along the path made of pebbles he sees the woman and man joining a larger group, one of them to the rear notices Cooper and waves him down in rushed succession.

Hmmmm,

he thinks, well they would be afraid if it was him causing this rush, unlikely they had found out about his late-night supper blood bath. It usually took a couple of days before they would declare anyone missing or dead usually blaming a runaway or rival clan. So he skipped on down the path in anticipation to see what was going on. He arrives at the edge of the path to see a familiar face, Ethel, an old woman in her seventies, he had once thought about tearing her arm completely off and eating it in front of her while she bleeds out, simply because she is the village nose and her voice cuts through his mind like butter, but she makes the best soup he has ever tried, so he has left her alone for now. He moves next to her.

"ethel dear what's happening "he says while peering over the crowd "

She turns to him and smiles in a way he doesn't quite like too much. admiration there, if only she knew what he really would like to do to her!

"it's wee Katie, Cooper, her father hasn't seen her in hours she headed out to the forest and hasn't been seen for hours we be expecting the worst for the wee soul "

She says in a sweet wee voice and in a way of pessimism

they had never notice this quick before, what was different about this time. Had he slipped up? Left some sort of clue? But he had been so careful, now a look of concern moves over his slim pale face "that's awful, how can he possibly sleep, he must beside himself. I met her recently, such a nice girl, but how can they be sure she's just no ran off or is playing a game of some kind "he said sighing

"ahh you see normally that would be the case, but she hasn't just left, there's some

evidence of foul play "

She says while raising her head dissatisfaction

"evidence" Cooper gulps

She turns back to him

"yes, a piece of tartan caught an a sharp branch, from the look of the colour it's from one of the eastern clans, possible mc Kenzie's"

That look of relief moves back over Cooper as he lets out a small smile. What a stroke of luck, he thinks ,that on the same moment he slaughters a girl some old piece of tartan merges in to the crime scene and becomes his saviour. Unknown to him that jimmy had fabricated the whole tartan. The story just to relax Cooper and subdue him. The whole town is now there, all standing round yet there was no tartan, the only evidence was poor Jimmy's eye, witnessing the butchering of his own offspring, but the only people that know this now is Jimmy and Daniel. He thought alerting the whole town would have given away the game. Everybody starts to move into the church and take seats. Cooper sits straight right at the front as if he ruled the village. Daniel and Jimmy stare quickly at each in disgust, then quickly look away again, so as not to give the game away. Somehow a deep black crow has also made it in the room and is flapping aimlessly around searching for exit, but eventually admits defeat and perches on a wooden beam above the main alter and observes the crowd like somewhat of a grand mister .There is distant and vague chatter amongst the crowd. Zek stands up to the podium and raises his hand, all the peoples chatter disappears slowly, gradually then there is silence

Zek speaks

"There has been a gross murder of one of our own, young Katie Jimmy's daughter she has been missing for some time now and we have found some blood where she was last seen. There was also a tag of tartan from one of the eastern clans, this could explain all the missing people, they bastards from the east "

several spurt out abuse from the crowd, Cooper smiles downwards, while thinking to himself, that all some kilted moron had to take a stroll through this land catching his tartan on a tree of a branch and bought him all this free time to eat the rest of the people from this village, and the neighbouring clans while they blame each other, yes his food source had just increased massively. Yet he does not know that the leaders are conspiring, plotting to their very hearts against him.

after much debate from the villagers Zek speaks a final plan

"Right bring in the chest "

Jiminy and Daniel heave in a giant chest and place it on the floor, they all look at it in amazement, Cooper peers forward in curiosity, what had these monkeys came up with?

"the plan is that we mount this chest on a cart, then we drive it with horses toward them. Then when it hits their village, our new cocktail of oils will blow with a short fuse. Timing will be everything. Cooper looks amazed that these primates could have devised such a plan. He was really impressed and was going to play along, he sniggered in his head

. wow there's some hope for this species after all

Zek stands proud at their achievement

"right people, here are the order of things, all people please return safely to your homes "

The entire church rises and moves, Cooper goes to rise and move towards the exit, Zek places his hand on his shoulder.

"Cooper you are the only person I, we all trust to look after the device until we return. I discussed it with Jimmy, he trusts you almost as much as I do. Please guard the chest, we will return in Twenty minutes to load it on to a cart"

Cooper smiles in satisfaction

"yes this is something I can most definitely do, always happy to help my old friend "

Cooper says in a reassuring tone. Ok, so they were well sucked in ha-ha not much to do now but watch them fight it out.

He sits back and casually puts his mud covered shoes with disrespect up on the church benches and relaxes his neck.

All village elders leave, and it all goes silent for a minute.

Next minute SMASH BANG BANG BANG CLINK CLINK

Cooper lifts his head what the fuck was that? he looked round the light had changed, instead of the white sunny pouring light funnelling through the six rectangle windows, there was nothing but blackness, there had been some kind of thick wooden covers moved over them. His eyes re adjusted and now he could see that there was pulley system that had released these covers and then wedges, made from iron, that had permanently fallen holding the thick covers in place. Next his pinpoint ears hears voices outside the big wooden doors, he hears wood being fixed and hammered across them. nails starting to protrude on the back of the doors, then he hears jimmy talking to Zek.

"I'm sorry Zek but we had to let everyone think it wasn't him, if he had got a whiff of what was going on, he would have never come. He's a monster an unnatural beast! I watched him kill my …. Katie"

 he says between sobs

"NOW THAT BASTARD will pay"

A cold fear filled coopers entire being, realising he has been duped by a bunch of simple village folk. He stands up slowly and growls and looks round, his eyes shimmer green and glance for an exit. Next, he hears a speech outside from Zek, followed by a dull mutter of lots of voices, he runs up to the now bolted, Shut doors and listens

"This monster has been living among you, feeding, killing and taking your loved ones away. He has been pulling the wool over our eyes even I did not suspect till jimmy told me the truth, a man I can only trust over all words "

the speech is interrupted, on many occasions, by anger and disbelief. Comments from the crowd that all lead to the same chant from all,

"BURN HIM"

"BURN HIM"

"BURN HIM "

Cooper now seems very concerned, he hears a voice now directed at him, its Jimmy

"COOPER, we do out know how long you've been doing this or how many of my people you have killed and eaten but no more, NO MORE!!!

Jimmy punches the door with his bare hand. Cooper decides that speaking, At this point will only escalate their anger, so he keeps searching for exit, with no success.

He finds a floor based trap door leading to storm exit, but it has been sealed shut by Jimmy and Daniel with metal beams. How could he have missed all this, how could a creature of his extraordinary years be so easily overcome, sloppy that's what. He thought he had been so careful but obviously not well at all! Not ever again, if I get out of this mess I'm being much more careful, much more tactful.

He sniffs and , then sniff again twice this time, whipping round, to his horror he can now see flames and white smoke appearing on the door, also now smoke from the window covers.

Fuck, there burning him, Cooper heals from most things fast, but a whole body flaming not so much! He runs at the door but it's now flaming too hot to even approach never mind breaking it. He fumbles around in circles trying to find way to escape the smoke getting even more dense. He hears the village people chanting a prayer to their lord. He looks at the chest he was charged with guarding and opens it, oh no, he thinks it's full of some kind of flammable oil. If the fire reaches this, he would be a goner. Next something bright appears above him, he slowly looks up, a roof beam it's on fire, he runs to the other end of the church and watches. He must surely be screwed here. Next the beam falls in, a colossal inferno of fire, Cooper covers his face, ok this is it he thinks to himself, game over, no more cooper. He pulls back when he uncovers his face, there is shock, the beam has smashed through the wooden floor and left a massive hole right next to the sealed trapdoor. Surely not, he could not be this lucky, he runs at his top speed and flees down the hole before the flames can even extend on to his clothes. He suddenly realises he was not successful, he was on fire, his entire back had caught alight, he lets out a high-pitched squeal. He is met by a tunnel only fit for crawling. He crawls and crawls and finally comes out about ten meters from the torched church, coughing and spluttering, he rolls around until the flames extinguish, he sits for ten minutes. and just looks up at the sky then drags himself in to a formation of bushes to repair and hide .

Back at the village the fire has burned away all that is burnable and all that remains is stone and ash jimmy and Zek begin poking the embers to look for signs he got out.

"look Zek its still sealed"

 pointing at the make shift seal he had created to seal the hatch and all metal window spikes intact.

" he's gone the bastard "

they all do several more checks to ensure Coopers demise, then start moving away from the church, they had won! Against an immortal creature

 HOW wrong they were!

<u>Chapter 12 the beginning of the end</u>

Kevin breaks his mind out of a sleep that came from nothing but pure rage and adrenalin depletion. His eyes try to focus but even though he had not consumed any alcohol he felt the effects of a hangover. Finally some degree of focus, a metal toilet, no toilet seat just crude slats of wood in its place. The floor a solid colour of grey badly painted with some kind of cheap floor paint . the Concrete walls painted as well, but cheap plaster, the kind with the holes that feed back in to the wall like swiss cheese. He knew exactly where he was , a flood of memories shoot back , getting fingerprinted, swabbed in his mouth and body searched. Also attending a very bored doctor, who without Kevin even asking, was given two blue Valium that he was quite happy to swallow. There's a clink on his big sealed metal door of the cell.   A horror like eye appears at a small, side to side, slide hole. It scans the room, then moves on to Kevin, then scans up and down like a robot laser. After seeing there is no threat, the door it grinds open and a man walks in the cell. To kevs astonishment, not a uniformed officer, the imposter speaks in a soft voice

"hi there Kevin I'm DC Davidson C.I. D we just want to ask you a few questions "

Kevin looks confused

"hey I'm sorry about the tattie guy I just lost it you know"

Kevin replies

"it's not just about that Kevin we just want a little chat "

DC Davidson says in that soft voice, the kind of voice that's trying to convince Kevin he's safe and that this man is his friend. But Kevin knew better, this wasn't his run in with the police and that talk was not going to be nice like the little soft voice

Kevin gulps

"ok"

He stands up and follows the DC, he's led to a room, he thinks, should I get a lawyer? But then thinks ahhh, I only shouted I never hit anyone, so he thinks he can wing it. The room has a school desk in it with a tape recording device on it, there is already a man sitting in the room he looks like a fatter run-down version of john Travolta. The first DC ushers kevs to a blue plastic seat, he already can see this is going to be a cliché good cop bad cop situation. How sad Kevin thinks that only happened in the movies surely

The fat Travolta talks

"let's talk about robbery KEVIIN "

Ok now a little bit panic sets in on Kevin. These freaks are either bored just playing games, or even worse trying to pin something he never done on him!

"robbery what robbery "

Kev says confused

The DC looks at him in disgust as if he should know every little in and out

"ok KEVIN do you know the king family "

Now Kevin really confused he has no clue what this about

"no, I have not a clue what you're on about "

Kevin insists

The fat Travolta stands and throws a pile of paperwork in kevs face and screams while pointing his finger "I know your involved you little cunt"

he then storms out the room

the other pc shakes his head

"let me help you, just tell the truth then we can all go home "

Kevin does not look convinced, he says nothing

"Ok back to you cell to see if a little time helps you remember "

He says, while taking kevs arm and escorting him back through walking past the other Travolta DC who looks like he went out the room and punched the wall about five times. Kevin looks at the floor and not him. They place Kev back in his cell and seal the metal door. He walks around the cell bored, he does sit-ups till he reaches four then realises he's not a boxer. He now gets a rush of adrenaline

"NO NO NO"

He shouts out loud.

They are not pinning this hit on him, they are not keeping him hear any longer, he kicks the wall like a super-hero like he could burst through it, but that doesn't happen it just send a thriving pain through his lower leg. Next there's that door clink again, it once again grinds open, this time a plain uniformed officer walks in. By this point Kevin is foaming in anger, fuelled by months of withdrawal, he turns round to look at him and the officer is dressed in completely in black and he has a bright, carrot coloured bush of hair and to match he also has a bright carrot ginger beard. Kev bursts into a fit of laughter and falls back on to his floor, based bed, every funny moment in his life had led here or perhaps his drug damaged mind was finally broken

The officer does not look best pleased.
"wooooaaa mate you're never going to or ever have had a girl in the sack hahahaha "

Kevin roars between laughs

He falls and continues roaring in laughter, the ginger officer then takes a large bag of chips in white paper bag and a Twix and lays them on the floor behind him. He moves towards Kev, his face now the same colour of his beard and hair, he is almost grunting in anger. A second non-carrot coloured officer comes in behind him, they move on Kevin and both hold him down. Kevin tries his best to fight back but soon finds oud he is so much less powerful than these two non-heroin blazing police officers. They soon overpower him and hold his hands behind his back, the carrot officer leans down to his face and smiles he the grabs his lower lip and squeezes it with both thumbs, this is a shock to Kev the pain is unreal, sharp.

"now your screaming like a girl, little man "

The offices says while squeezing even harder ,they flip Kev over and lay him on his back,, they rip his shirt down and the other officer kneels on his arms to free up his own arms, he then puts his hand in to a double knuckle and starts rubbing it horizontally across kevs collar bone, the pain is unbearable like someone operating on you without anaesthesia. It doesn't take long for Kev to pass out. He wakes up somewhat later dazed and confused and in the doctor's office again. The doctor is holding a blue gel pack on Kevin's chest. He looks down there is a huge purple and blue swell on his collar bone he closes his eye and a tear rolls out, he licks his lower lip as well and realises it's also swollen

BASTARDS he thinks

he asks the doctor if he's ok

"yes, son but trying to escape not a clever idea will only give them a reason to hurt you "

The doc says patiently.

Kev looks at him in astonishment

"are you serious I never done anything, just spoke, and they done this to me"

He says while further tears roll down his face the doctor looks at him in a bored non-caring manor

"to be honest we have three witnesses to say you made a move on an officer's weapon so they defended themselves "

Kevin goes to speak and then just puts his head down, how can he possibly defend against this, the word of three officers against little old Kev, a homeless, junk filled, using useless human being. He thinks about any kind of response then just submits to the doctor's checks. Then he Is escorted back to his cell. Tossing and turning trying to get some sleep. Before he knows it his cell light bursts in to a glorious blaze of artificial light then goes a clink of that incessant metal door, and one clothed officer comes in followed by a man with a g4s shirt on.

"right Kevin court time "

Kevin looks up as the officer says this, he stands to his feet and moves over to them, the g4s officer pushes forward a pair of bonded handcuffs, Kevin places his hands into them and they are snapped shut . And the g4s man holds them in the centre and starts pulling kevs along like a tamed donkey. Then they usher him down a long corridor where there is a man being dragged by two other officers except he's thrashing around like kite on a windy day, they purposely move Kevin in his direction then the clothed officer whispers on kevs ear.

"Remember this next time you think about breaking the law "

The out of control and obviously intoxicated stranger thrusts towards the small framed Kev

"what the fuck you looking at ye wee radge Il fuck you up prick, smash your teeth in CCCUUUNT "

The man drools, Kevin pulls back in fear as the stranger attempts to get at him, the g4s man keeps him moving forward towards another metal door with no eye hole and only one large handle, the g4s man lifts a fob to a plate on the wall and it bursts open the metal door and daylight pours in like fire, Kevin's eyes shrink to pin point pupils. He loses all colour to his sight but whites and basic greys his eyes burn like chemicals have been tossed in them , finally till they start to adjust . The first thing they focus on is a large van bearing the same g4s logo. He is ushered in to a booth with a small windows in, then is sat down. The g4 man shuts the door three quarters then reaches in, he pulls Kevin's hands out of the gap and removes this cuffs. Everyone who watches a movie where hand cuffs are removed thinks that look of relief and rubbing of the wrists is fake and put on, wrong! It's the best feeling in the world and the relief is pure euphoria, Kevin does this ritual and sits down his door bolts shut behind him, then he hears a various amount of prisoners being led in and fitted in to their small rooms. He even hears the crazy bastard that tried to kill him in the corridor. The engine ignites underneath him and the large human carrying unit begins to move, he looks out his small window in his booth ,he noticed it was blacked out from the outside and no one could see in ,only he could see nothing but things he was brought up with. A torture drive around the streets of childhood memories, the buildings he had been in and out of through his existence, all the better and good memories of time passed basically gone, not here now. It was like a small window in to the past, a window only he can see out and no passers-by can see the end result of this miserable existence.

The van moves down a cobbled street, Kev sees a bar

THE OZ BAR

his memory searches back to a wake for his uncle Stewart, where he got too drunk on the free alcohol and made an embarrassment of himself. He thinks on how he would have changed that event and made it more pleasant. He was full of regrets like this. He contemplates daily on events changing from bad too good wishing he had done it all different. He lowers his head in sadness because there is no going back, there is no change, there is only now and next. The van slows, and from the corner of his window he can see a large metal door sliding upwards, then the van moves in slowly and bypasses the large door, in the same manor it grinds down again, and seals them off from the world. Then Kevin hears the g4 officers approaching, his small door opens and the handcuffs appear in front of him again. Kevin, in routine, now pushes his hands out again. They snap shut, the door fully opens and Kevin is lead out, then after being lead down a masonry stone corridor he reaches a long line of large steel prison cells, all occupied in high numbers. They move Kevin in to a cell containing one large man twice the size of Kevin, the man is wearing leather trousers and a tight white tee-shirt. As soon as Kevin enters the cell he looks down to the back wall and sees a metal hole in the wall, he immediately knows it's for urinating in. As soon as Kevin sits in the cell, the man looks at him, then starts doing press up's on the floor, Kevin pulls back uneasy ,he then jumps up and does fifteen star jumps, and after that spends the next two hours explaining to Kev how to dismantle a m-17 machine gun. Kevin finds each ten minutes of the conversation more disturbing, each step of the way, and eventually just ends up nodding at him in agreeance. He is also slowly noticing that each name is being called , one at a time, to speak to their lawyer, Kevin is just slowly praying in his head that the next name is his! At last, after two hours of talk about high grade military weaponry, his name is called and a g4 officer collects him and leads him through to a room entirely made of glass with a blue metal table in the middle, it was a very intimidating room, like the movie where you see the five people behind the blacked out glass window observing a crazy serial killer while he picks his teeth, thinking it's a mirror. The door buzzes and a very tired looking lawyer in a black suit enters and without even looking at Kev sits down and starts looking at a file

"hmmmm Kevin ii can get the assault dropped and a fine applied if you admit guilt and it will go on your record as disturbing the peace …if you don't, I think, we will struggle to get bail out of fear of reprisal. so the judge will apply a custodial remand until your trial and I think the waiting time is about 3 months So I would advise you plead guilty and take the fine. Worst case some small community service"

He says still not looking at him as if he were not a human being. Instead a large file sitting in this chair, an ornamental outcome of the lawyers existence serving low intelligence criminals

Kevin looks at him for a minute and then comes to a decision he was a junkie.homeless.friendless.no girlfriend, no future.

 The last thing he could think of now is being imprisoned in saughton prison for three months, now that would not do at all. He eventually agrees with lawyer and asks him for assurance he won't get jail time. His lawyer confirms defiantly a fine. Kevs head rests easier, he's taken back to his urine cage where to his pleasure the crazy gunman is being led out to his lawyer. Kev takes this time to collect himself he lays across the whole bench on the cell and closes his eyes, blurs of colour and flashes enter his vision, he manages to enter some form of sleep even if just for a few minutes. That's enough to help the morning he is having, things go dark for a while.

He is woken by someone calling out to him

"ee ooooii wee man oooii you heyheyHEY "

Kevin turns around and see a man in a opposite cell

"I what's up "

Kevin said still completely unaware of reality after emerging from his power nap

"ye got any tobacco"

Kevin wipes his eyes

"naw mate I smoked my last before they brought me here "

Kevin forces out of his brain

The man looks down and raises his face in a rage of pure insanity like Dr Jeckell transforming in to Mr Hyde and starts spitting in kevs direction

"you little cunt ill smash your fuckin teeth down your throat I know you got baccy I'm going to find you in the clink and bite your fuckin nose off cuuuuunt "

He screams while trying to force his face through the bars like he could melt between them

Kevin looks uneasy and now just turns away from him and looks at the urinal he can hear him screaming in the back ground then some relief his name is called again, and he is again ushered by the g4 security officers this time up a stair case he reaches a wooden door and then next as the officer opens it he hears his name being called

"CASE 16651728

Kevin is pulled through a wooden door and it explodes with artificial light and burns the retinas out his eyes after being in a cell for hours then to be thrust in to this light it is surreal once his eyes adjust he realises that there are about thirty sets of eyes on him all behind him the level of uneasiness increases beyond control a small trickle of sweat drips down his neck, suddenly all motor function seize and he becomes as stiff as a board. Panic sets in, it becomes harder and harder to concentrate on anything. His vision moving from thing to thing and suddenly it focuses on the judge, big thick rimmed glasses, white hair pushing out from his already white wig. His clothes perfectly ironed even his cuffs look ironed, no laptop, no digital recorder, just a pencil and paper... By Christ, in fact now on closer inspection three perfectly sharpened pencils sitting in place in a polished cup. Oh my god Kevin was screwed this judge was going to hate everything about him. Nothing he said or done was going to make a difference, he was going to burn for attacking the little old potato man! Kevin's life was over good and done, he looks at his lawyer in the hope that he looks confident... wrong, the poor man looks folded from the case before. His appears to almost be shaking, and the judge seems to be staring at him with what can only be contempt and dislike for Kevin's lawyer. That fear Kevin has felt for weeks on a certain level of the scale jumps up a notch.

"Now Mr Bradsheen, can you please explain to me why your client took it upon himself to attack a defenceless shop keeper and cause nearly five hundred pounds in damages? "

The judge bellows without even looking at Kevin or his lawyer instead looking at his prized pencils Kevin looks at the floor and sighs.

"WELL......"

The judge says, while the lawyer is overlooking a note of paper

"Your honour my client was suffering from a massive withdrawal of opium and was grieving a family loss coupled with sleep deprivation and alcohol abuse, he has expressed his deepest regrets and wishes he could take back the incident, as he was merely trying to seek employment. "

The judge looks at him for a second

"Carry on"

He says in a calmer voice

"Your honour, my client has no previous history of violent crime and has been in good behaviour for considerable time, I request that he be allowed out on bail or he is willing to plead guilty if this matter is resolved today and no longer waste the courts time. "

The judge grabs another piece of paper and goes quiet for several minutes.

This makes Kevin feel incredibility unstable and nervous, as if they are deciding a death row verdict. Finally, the Judge talks "Mr Bradsheen, I happen to be a friend of the owner of this shop and although your client's record has some bad marks on it, I am willing to be lenient this time due to the fact he has not been trouble for some time. I am imposing a deferred sentence of six months custodial imprisonment. Where in this time we will review your client's behaviour?"

The judge says in a calm collected voice and strikes a small hammer on his desk.

A small thinner gentleman stands up and repeats the judge's verdict out loud.

Mr Bradsheen turns to Kevin and smiles in a satisfied manner, Kevin does not seem impressed he thinks in his own head, What the Human FUCK!!!! That is not a fine, that is a joke he told me a fine. Now for the next six months I must be Invisible. How the hell can I do this? While being homeless, friendless, and on heroin. This is a task unachievable in such a big city. Although, he was just happy not to be incarcerated. Kevin's thoughts for the last two hours were that he was going to jail, no matter what but, now he was free. Free to fuck it all up again!

The thin man stops talking and the G4 security officer tugs on Kevin's handcuffs to usher him away, back through the varnished door, back to the cells. They put Kevin in a cell at the end of the row on his own. Not with the tobacco psycho, not with the gun maniac, just all on his own. At last, a piece of good luck.

Kevin waits for what feels like hours, but, was probably about an hour. When your awaiting something as special, as your own release, that changes all the rules. Finally, one of the g4 officers calls his name and takes him to a small grey desk, he hands him a piece of card to sign, Kevin doesn't even read it he just signs, it could be a document to end his life by firing squad he doesn't care. He just wants his freedom. The officer hands him a bag full of Kevin's stuff, including shoes and his jacket. Kevin slips his jacket on and slides in to his shoes

"try and behave son "

The officer directs at Kevin, he nods back in agreeance, but to be honest he would donate a kidney right now if it would gain his freedom. The officer unlocks a small metal door attached to the previous large roller door and lets Kevin through. The smell of freedom hits him fast, somehow the air tastes better, even though Kevin can smell himself, the air tastes sweet and clean. He quickly rushes in a fast pace along the cobbled road to ensure his escape, he knows his time is limited there could only be one out come from this, only one resolve, back to jail for Kevin. There's no way that he could continue in Edinburgh, he had to escape, or he was fucked good and proper, but how? He has no clothes or money. He heads along the cobbled road and takes a sharp left and starts ascending a road, towards the famous Greyfriars Bobby. A famous statue of a dog Kevin had no idea why. As he approaches the dog. There are several Chinese tourists surrounding it, all gasping and flashing cameras in a tourist like fashion. Kevin muddles in between them, now in a state of curiosity about the dog he sees a plaque. It reads ......**John Gray, who worked for the church as a night-watchman. When John Gray died he was buried in Greyfriars Kirkyard, the kirkyard. Surrounding in the Old Town of Edinburgh. Bobby then became known locally, spending the rest of his life sitting on kirkyard surrounded by his master's grave.**

Kevin feels satisfied that he has found this out about the dog. After years of passing it and not really giving a shit to find out but at the same time he couldn't care less right now. He turns to walk away, back to his miserable life, but as he turns, he sees a purple and pink purse hanging out the corner of one of the Chinese tourist's bag. A feeling of evil/guilt overwhelms Kevin, should he do it? should he be the good man here and just tell her? His head fills with reasons to support both causes, but then the tie breaker INSURANCE ... That's how he was going to justify this horrible act, she was a tourist and therefore will have travel insurance and will recover from this. Without a second thought Kevin slides his dirt covered hand in to the side pouch and takes the purse!! He turns fast and speeds away from the scene of the crime. He walks for what seems like ages. He finally reaches a stone lane, he goes down the steep stone stairs until he reaches a doorway recess. As he enters it the smell of urine overwhelms him but, he doesn't care it was time to investigate his find. The risk was massive, just out of jail ten minutes and already he had committed a crime outside the very court that had just seen fit to release him. Kevin opens the purse zip first to see an array of Scottish coins, nothing dazzling probably about seven pound all in change. He then gets a feeling of disappointment realising if that's all the coins she had, then the notes weren't going to be ample either. He whips the purse open fast to find out quickly the result, like ripping of a band aid fast ...WOW, OH MY GOD, WOW, WOW ... A rush of adrenaline fills Kevin and he paces back and forth fast while looking at what he had uncovered. A stack of bank notes twenty's and tens, he looks away and then looks back ... yep still there! He calms down, then counts the find. Two hundred and ninety pounds in notes and seven pounds in change. The girl must have just been to a bank machine, WOW … Kevin removes the money and stuffs the purse in to a bin, just opposite his doorway and heads down to the bottom of the lane. Kevin suddenly has a thought it was time to escape Edinburgh, there was too much risk here, too much possibility of getting put back in jail. There was only one hope –

THE HIGHLANDS

Chapter 13 up north

There was a chance he could live up there free of drugs, free of judgement, a fresh start, a new hope, new future "A chance "

He comes out the alley into an array of black taxi's, all competing to squeeze into the already small Taxi rank, an array of selfish taxis blocking everyday traffic. People beeping horns,

People getting out of cars and shouting, a completely different scene of what he was going to get in the Scottish Highlands. No, it was going to be different up there a clean green paradise. Free from the temptations of this big city, he pushes through the madness of taxi land and squeezes past all the enraged traffic and in to the train station.

It reads Waverly train station, Welcome to Edinburgh. He sneers at the welcome sign and walks on past towards his new life, confident of the future that awaits him. He heads along a Metal passageway until he reaches a staircase, he makes his way down. The poles of the staircase are made of green metal. Worn and tattered like an old truck, green colour replaced by Chips of dark rust. As he approaches the bottom of the stairs, a man wearing a tweed jacket, gravitates towards him. In the corner of his vision a train departs, slowly moving at first then gaining speed, moving further and further away. Kevin doesn't know which way to Look, The tweed man? or the departing train? His drug fuelled eyes concentrate on the man, the man looks Concerned! He shuffles past quicker. He continues his route until he reaches a glass Doorway. As he approaches it, it opens in a mechanical Manner. He walks through to discover himself in a Marks and Spencer's store. Suddenly fear and torment from the Tesco experience came rushing back and he does not wish to relive that nightmare. He moves quickly passed to find himself in a large room with seats in the middle and further glass doors to the other side. It feels like he has a row of people watching him, all set up just for him. Every kind of person moving from a railway station to another location, all aimed on him!

Kevin feels very uneasy and decides to ignore the entire situation. Quickly, he moves through the Second set of glass doors and finds himself in a large ticket distribution room. There are four clerks and five Large machines, he moves towards one of the machines and it states – GNER rail

Press start on the screen, he is about to push the button, suddenly it all becomes blurred, he can't even see a single word. Sleep deprivation combined with drug fuelled rage - including alcohol, combined with everything on this horrible day rolled into one nightmare of a situation! You just simply could not work technology!

Now he joins a three-person Queue, in front of the kiosks he finds himself to be even more un easy when he realises that a police officer is standing beside him, at the entry to the kiosks, he decides to Ignore him, as well as the three person Queue. In this kind of state, it feels like an eternity!

At last he was next. Sweat pouring from his forehead, all oxygen had been removed from the room and all that was left was the oxygen surrounding his lips!

He shuffles to the kiosk stating number four, the woman looks at him in disgust. You can always hide your appearance when you're tired and fatigued but, after a four-week, two-day long period of drug fuelled binge, hiding your Appearance is not easy!

"Can I help you Sir? "

She says in disgust

"I would like one ticket to Inverness please, no return "

Kevin says to her, as if she knows his entire life story. What is a junkie wasting her time for? She thinks.

"Will that be first class sir?"

She says in a condescending manner

"Yes, yes it will be first class "

Kevin sits back in a smug Manner, directs his hand into his pocket and reveals a pile of notes, she was surprised that he had any money at all!

"Okay, that will be forty-seven pounds and twenty pence please "

Kevin counts out two twenty-pound notes and the ten-pound note and then hands them to her, she takes them as if she has just been handed her own money that he had stolen from her!

 Then, hands him some black and orange tickets and looks at him without even saying thanks.

Kevin doesn't even care, nice people were awaiting him, it was time to move on, time to start a new life, time for a fresh start in the Highlands. He walks away from the kiosk, without returning the thank you either, then back to the glass doors quickly avoiding the police officer and quickly avoiding the people who are viewing him like cattle. Onto a third set of doors to venture out into the open train world. Each person that meets his field of view onset with purpose, all with their own dedicated agenda.

All he could see was trains, this is what was an endless track taking away from this place, this place that had taken his life and cost him so much, and caused him so much misery and disgust, this place that taken his life and turned into a drug fuelled mess. This will be his future, this will be his change. Even if it was with ill-gotten gains. He looks up at the big yellow and black board with the train numbers on it. then once again his vision plays tricks it becomes a blurred smudge of orange mixed into black, while at the same time pulsing like a heart. Damn how would he ever find his train? But then, in the corner of his eye is a small kiosk labelled

INFORMATION

Saviour…. He was surprised to see that there was nobody in front of him, there was a pleasant man waiting for him. A quiet small fellow, wearing a blue jacket stating GNER not condescending like the previous woman, the man smiles and greets him politely

"how may I help you young man "

He says in a friendly inviting voice

"I'm looking for the next train to Inverness I have a first-class ticket "

Kevin says proudly

the man looks down that small screen

"hmmmmm your train leaves in twenty minutes from platform six I would just go now if I was you"

Kevin Nods at him and smiles back

"thanks mate"

Kevin looks for platform six somewhere in his head smudged vision he sees a large six, the train is sitting nicely waiting for him, it looks like a golden chariot gleaming red and white, with a sticker showing a picture of a sunset birthday in to a field of vegetables, this would take him to paradise away from all this crime drugs and failure. He walks towards the first-class section holding his ticket high and proudly, nobody pays any attention to him at all. He approaches the door He sees a large a luminated button solid silver in the middle with the glowing orange band. He pushes the orange disk and the door hisses then a mechanical noise almost a pressure release it slides open like a door from a si-fi space ship. He walks in Slowly not quite sure what to expect, after all everything today has been a disaster why not this train as well. He turns into his carriage, to his surprise - Best seats EVER! They are fantastic, covered in beautiful red leather ordained in the GNER logo. He wanders for a second looking for his number, He finds his Seat it's a single unit and it has a lovely cover on it, also in a nice red This was going to be some journey, on a level Kevin had never experienced before, he was excited

"Hello Sir, can I offer you a cold drink "

Kevin Look up startled there is a large man standing there with a trolley

"How home much is it"

Kevin fumbles

"Why It's free young man you are in first class "

"Would you like a biscuit or a packet of crisps as well"

He proceeds to say

I whiskey is free?

Kevin asks

"why yes, it is"

the man says back

Kevin's eyes enlarge, what you get free food and drink on this 1st class this could not be true? Surely stealing one person's wallet could not have not resulted in this great lifestyle?

Oh my God he was here, the start of his New life

"yes please, I will have a whiskey and two packets of crisps"

Kevin says he slides back into his new seat and relaxation floats about his body, he takes a deep breath and a sigh of relief AHAHAHAHH...

He hears some whistle outside the train, Then the doors Seal shut, and the train starts to slowly move away. At last, freedom away from this rancid city. The train gains more and more speed and the engine sound intensifies into a soft purr. He is now seeing all his childhood memories flying past the window behind him. As he watches his childhood memories disappear one by one. he reaches a large metal bridge! It's the road road bridge, you can see it just in the distance as the train gradually turns a corner, there is a second airy bridge, a large metal bridge criss-crossing design dull red in colour nothing like the glorious red on the train seats , this bridge a thing of beauty. A large monstrosity of mankind not made to resemble something of nature's beauty or intricacies that is of a plant. But instead, a mish mash of steel and strength bent in to shape for the purpose of cars, Trains, even foot passengers. These were all good things in Kevin's eyes.

Now that he had his motivation towards new life, he could sit back and relax and enjoy the things that he'd ignored. There is no place in his life for drugs, no reason to further abuse alcohol into the system, he is better than that now, yes, the future After they leave the bridge. The train enters an intricate coastline of beautiful beaches and that weaves in and out, eventually ending up into countryside. green long fields, as far as the eye can see. Cows standing pointlessly in order, sheep, blots of white colour in the Greenfields resemble the white dots on a domino. Kevin feels his eyes getting heavier and heavier, a mix of the free food and drink is received nicely. Suddenly he loses all consciousness and moves to another reality, somewhere that you're not supposed to be. Train moves quietly and slowly shaking his brain back and forth. The world has become a twisted dark reality in his head, deeper, deeper into his head, like an episode from Fantasia all colours jumping around in his mind that shouldn't be there in the drug-based reality. All was dark and now his new life awaits

....

Chapter 14 the massacre

steam rises slowly from Coopers back, the ground around him
Scorched, as he struggles to lift his hands to raise his body. He
manages to turn his head and look back at a black cloud emanating
from the church behind him. It is dark plume still visible bursting out
of the ground like a mushroom into the open sky. He manages to roll
his body over, how Could they have done this? He feels outsmarted.
Where had he gone wrong? he was being so blasé, so relaxed about
his killing, that he had got sloppy you had! He must have missed
something but what could he have missed? He concludes it must have
been his recent kill, must have been jimmy's daughter. Suddenly
something changes he starts feeling something he hadn't had to feel
for a long time, anger, pure anger, revenge. HOW DARE THEY. He
could not let these simple creatures walk around pretending they
were better than him. He would have his revenge. But first anyone,
anything, just to help him get him on his feet you must feed, feed
urgently he must!

Jimmy sits down at his chair and gives a long sigh of relief, he falls
back into it like a sack of potatoes. He looks at the wall at a large cast
woven tapestry, his daughter had put into place for him she flashes
into his memory, smiling. A tear runs down his face followed by
another and another. His hands move to the table, then to the side of
the chair, where he pulls out a knife, encased in leather. He pulls to
unveil the knife and puts it to his throat and starts counting down
slowly while tears pour down his face TEN,NINE,EIGHT,SEVEN,SIX,FIV-
--------SMASH his front door explodes to reveal a flash of light, a large
figure flies in and pins him to his chair before he gets a chance to
scream. A bony wet hand covers his mouth, muffling his screams as
he tries to focus on what is happening. To his terror Cooper Is
standing in front of him, his face Charred and burned bits of skin
falling off his face. As they look at each other in disgust, his pointing
the red in his eyes intensifies and evil is truly realised. He takes one
last look at the tapestry on the wall before Coopers dark teeth sink

into his face. Blood splatters everywhere, exploding from every inch of his face, his daughters' tapestry on the wall covered and splattered with dark red blood. Cooper sooks and sucks all the blood coming from his face, drawing every inch of it into his being like energy pulsing from a broken power line. Jimmy's body twitches and thrives the pain unbearable to live with, in his mind he just looked for death. He has lost his daughter, he has lost a battle, his one task accomplished killing Cooper, a failure now! to top it all off he has an immortal creature tearing his face to pieces.

Cooper steps back slowly, jimmy gurgles, the pain becoming less and less, his heart becoming slower and slower until nothing, no beating, no pain. He looks at katies tapestry and smiles, Cooper throws his dead body to one side he throws his body back and screams, the scream echoes from glen to glen and birds flock away from tress in succession .He takes a moment, half bent over and lets Jimmy's blood coarse round his veins and let the weakness pass but it wasn't enough, he had been instantly repaired, It still wasn't enough that he could make a clean getaway. But These fools had to be taught a lesson They had to be punished, He was maybe the only one of his kind, but he was better than them! Stronger, faster and smarter.

As Cooper peers Through Jimmy's broken door he sees someone, Keith, he's a local, must have heard something come to see what the noise was. He straightens up in and lunges through the door and straight at Keith, he pushes his long Bony fingers through his eye's sockets, the poor unexpecting Keith lets out a small Yelp and he falls to the ground and dies instantly. He looked around him there is no one else in there. He spends the next twenty-five minutes moving from small neighbours on the outskirts, tearing them apart in horrible and disgusting ways. He takes the leg from his last victim and places it over his shoulder as a gift for the next house. This house was a special house, this house was Daniel's house. He knocks on the door. From the other side of the door there is a soft voice.

"Hello who is it "

A nervous whisper utters

"It's Jimmy I'm here to celebrate "

Cooper has, of course, mimic the voice not very well, I may add. The door opens slowly, before it even passes the first inch, a super smash opens it at the speed of light. Poor Daniel is thrown backwards across His little home like a piece of paper. Cooper casually places the leg in front of him in the middle of the hall. Fear fills Daniels face, he had messed up, somehow, he had stopped cooper but somehow, he had forgotten something. He would never know what Cooper had done to escape. In-fact he would never find out anything ever again! Punishment would be bestowed upon him he kicks the leg over and slowly starts walking towards Daniel.

"So, you thought you could Trap me My BOY! you thought that you insignificant little creatures could beat me, you thought that no matter what you did I would never get out that flawless TRAP! Wow who is sitting on the floor now, who is trapped with no escape who will die slowly, but I laugh! You're my little pig, now which little piggy shall we start with?"

 Cooper floats slowly across the floor and grabs Daniel's hand

"this little piggy went to the market"

As he says that snaps off a finger, Daniel screams in pain

"and this little piggy went to……"

 And Snap another finger off,

"oh no look behind me Daniel what's on the middle of the floor DANIEL?

He looks and there's nothing.

"OK about the little piggy need to leave the house before the time Daniel has time to protest, he snaps off his next finger,

"look again Danny boy"

He peers round in agony hoping it will prevent anymore fingers getting pulled off, It's a human leg!

"yes, I want to do to see the end result, I'm going to snap you into pieces one at a time. I gave jimmy a quick death on account of Jimmy's daughter, I gave him a quick pass, also I needed his blood quick"

Cooper says, while staring in to his teary, terror filled eyes

"please what can, please help me, someone help me "

Daniel blubbers, as his hands pour with blood

You made the trap, I'm going to take you apart piece by piece, everybody you've ever known. Is going to be taken apart piece to piece. Daniel's eyes open wide and the tall, dark figure, pure evil, starts walking, he gets larger and larger until there's nothing but Daniels screams. He, one by one wakes up each part of the village, Death is spread's far and wide and hard, but no one escapes, no pets, no people, no homes.

Zach looks around him there is nothing but burning buildings and bits of the people he loved scattered around him, there's no more tears left, just a once proud town leader, a broken man trying to crawl away as he is impaled in both legs with what seems to be wooden shards.

"Oh, Zekky!"

he turns back to look at the evil cooper pursuing him

"Copper please, I'm the last from this village, there will be nothing left of us, no stories. As if we didn't exist, he flashes forward and pushes another shark piece of wood through Zek's arm, he screams an evil scream to simulate Zek's pain and anguish. Zek screams in to the night air

"That's what I'm hoping Zachy boy no more talk of and it will look like another clan war, you predictable fools "

Zach closes his eyes; coopers long Bony fingers slide around his neck he smiles to the Sky and rip's his head off completely. he turns the head around and give is it a kiss and throws it into a fire, burning on the side of a building. He laughs again and turns to walk away Oh yes such a close call.......

But wait, this was it not real, something's, not right? He looked down to his body, it starts fading and disintegrating, fading away, suddenly he's lying on his back, what's happening?

"what the hell is happening to me?" then he realises this this was a reminiscent dream, this was nothing more than a dream to keep him sane. He looks down to realise he's back in the wooden box, back where they had imprisoned him, trapped in this nightmare, is there any hope for him? Anybody who could save him? Or was he to stay here for eternity with never again tasting hot wet delicious blood that he needs to feel alive, only time will tell. He had used up all the good thoughts in his brain, things   were getting more distant it was getting hard to remember things, what will become of him? After time his thoughts are becoming primal rage, rather than rational thought. He realises that the only thing left that he could move was his eyes, how long have you been down here? What could have caused such lengthened petrification? Could his brain still calculate the time, that it possible for him to get to the state, he forces the information out his dusty thoughts. NO it couldn't be ! Close to five hundred years.

This could be the end for him, no one will ever find him. He closes eyes and waits for them to turn to rock and Lie in eternal sleep dreaming of what was once and what will never be.

 Rest in peace Cooper but wait
…………………………………………………………………..

Chapter 15 The Inverness dream

A Large egg sits patiently waiting, he turns to his left, there is a drunken, unconscious golden nugget lying on the ground along with the happy teaspoon and a cornflake ball. Egg opens his large white and golden eyes and stretched long and hard, he shook Cornflake ball it too opened to Large set of eyes of its own, it looks to the large egg

"Oh God brother what have we done? How did we end up here "?

The egg looked disappointed

"I'll tell you what happened, you and spoon messed up, I don't blame nugget he was just following orders I can tell you now it's going to be a long time before bottle & caterpillar trust again"

Cornflake ball looks terrified

"what are we going to do, they going to kill us"

at this point the happy Spoon shakes awake as well

"Yo bro don't sweat it everybody makes mistakes"

the spoon says and looks confident in his new decision, nugget an egg look at them intensely! Spoon revises his statement

"Hmmmmm maybe some mistakes can't be helped or repaired "

Egg is about to respond, when suddenly a large Marmalade lid unscrews below them, and a skinny hairy caterpillar head pops out.

"Hello chaps Mr. bottle would like a word, perhaps you could bless him with your presence, you have some explaining to do"

Egg, spoon and nugget combined with Cornflake ball all look at each other in terror. Oh no, they all dropped into the opening where the lid had opened, it slides shut most immediately after they enter, they are confronted by a giant bottle, see through glass with a frosty blue colour and a plaque beside it stating

stand and pay homage before this glorious bottle

It turns around, it has a face, an angry face! big Scary large white eyes aimed on all four of them They all look at the magnificent bottle then gulp It begins to talk ……………….

Last stop for Inverness

All four of them look each other in surprise, they don't know what to say this was not a language that was used in the country, this was not a language they had ever heard before or any sort of sounds they were used too. it speaks again more anger in its eyes this time and louder.

Wake up This is the last stop for Inverness

The egg looks to nugget he is melting away into nothing, dissolving in front of is very eyes, reality breaking down. Something is destroying the world, he also looks to spoon, fear hits egg as he watches spoon slowly dissolve onto the ground into a puddle of Metallic nonsense. Surely not cornflake ball egg thinks, yes him too, his single pieces of cornflake expanding into individual pieces drifting away into nothing. What is happening, he thinks, egg looks at himself, his own body starting to dematerialise in front of him, he then see something in the distance, two large ovals opening, starting to reveal beams of light, what is happening? why is this happening to his home especially in such an important juncture in his career **Bang Bang dissolve me**

....
....

Kevin Awakes to a large woman standing over him, tapping a pen on a clipboard she looks confused

"yes, can I help you "

he says awkwardly

"I told you already you have fallen asleep this is the **last stop it is Inverness**"

He looks out the train window its pouring with rain. I'm going to want to go back to Edinburgh. he shakes his head NO NO then he stands up, make it today, his new start! He couldn't be here already how long have you been sleeping?? he thought.

He ignores the Women and carries on waking, he rubs his eyes and moves gradually more and more towards the already open train door. He walks out looking around and thinks his new life, his new world, a chance. He walks out in to his new gleaming paradise of shiny sunshine and opportunities. Hmmm, wait, he realises almost immediately, it's a rainy Drenched nightmare of concrete and metal. But OK this is only the train station, of course it would look like this, yeah ignore this situation. He carries on right past the train and walks to the end of the platform, this is it he thinks excitably as he walks through some doors and into his new universe of joy.

He's walks through the doors from the train station thinking to himself on How his life here would be so different to the one he had in Edinburgh, it had been a terrible existence, only here he could make a success of himself, suddenly his Chain Of thought is interrupted.

Suddenly his legs are tugged below, he turns around to see what it is.

"Hey buddy can you spare some change"

He is confronted by a dirty disgrace of a man, has clothes torn, his shoes split, sitting on a piece of dirty, urine-soaked cardboard.

Kevin is disgusted, a beggar in his new paradise, what was he doing here? Surely, he Had escaped from Edinburgh as well to start his own life but never quite got started. Unlike Kevin, who is going to succeed! Kevin doesn't even give him the time of day or look at him, he just walks away and makes him aware he's disgusted by him. Okay, he can accept this he thinks one problem easily done remove this from his thoughts and carries on. He walks along the high street of inverness to look and scope out a lay of the land. He reaches into his pocket to see how much money he has left, he decides the best course of action would be to try and find some sort of place to live. Two hundred and ten pounds, not bad that's what he had left, he could live with that,

The problem with drug abusers is that time becomes a freeze frame, reality life exists in the same era they started in and change becomes more difficult with every passing moment. Suddenly the possibility of two hundred and ten being a little amount of cash was no longer possible to Kevin in his head, this would buy him everything he needed, clothes, accommodation and probably a few nights out in posh restaurants, but of course he was still in a delusional state of mind. He looks to his left there is a Shop to his left **Primark.** He thinks, if he changes the look that he promotes, then it will lead to the House, job and ambition that he so desperately seeks. He walks into the store and is confronted by Three faceless mannequins, all three of the mannequins appear to be giving him a condescending look, upon him even though they're faceless, every part of them judging him convincing him to do better. Ignoring the three mannequins he proceeds directly to the male section of the store, he thinks, I mean, what do they know. He stretches forwards over a counter and grabs boxer shorts, extra small in size, he grabs socks a six pack of sport socks and begins browsing casually. A security guard has taken notice of him and is talking directly into a small receiver on his shoulder. He then proceeds to the clothes in corner of the store with a big ceiling hanging plaque stating MENS. he grabs new pair of jeans and then sees it, the perfect shirt, white with black trims. Truly this would bring him work, surely in his imagination he is floating round this store with elegance, and grace lifting each item with care and respect laying them down like feathers, but the hard reality he was an unwashed junkie alcoholic mess, reeking of all sorts and things pouring from his pores that not even he knows what it is , he was in complete imbalance and walking in a manner of pace rather than grace, speeding from rack to rack grabbing item after item messing up everything he touches with all the grace of a bull in a china store. But in kevs head all was good. This would give him the energy needed, everything without hesitation. Image was everything for him now, he goes to the checkout and pays, and he asks them if you can get dressed in the changing rooms, the store assistant. Looks reluctant but still agrees by nodding in the direction of the changing rooms. He floats in to the into the changing room, he drops his trousers quickly as soon as he gets in, looking around just in case anybody could see him through this cover that hangs over the changing room. I think it gives everybody the same feeling That they cover for changing doesn't quite cover you. He shrugs his shoulders and removes his top, he pulling the new clothes over his in sticky, sweaty body and hides all the travelling in one go, At last he was ready to start his new life, at last he was ready to escape the horribleness of his old city, where he had come from. Surely this outback city would have more of a lasting effect on him and promote change.? He could finally be somebody! Here he could be something! Not just a disgusting waste of human skin. He crushes his receipt and throws it into the corner of the changing room and walks out and proceeds to the exit, as soon as he is about to leave the store, a large hand places on his shoulder, he turns to see large gentleman, dark skinned creature of nature, a massive large skull and massive hands .

"Can I see a receipt please "

The monstrosity blurts

He must in a have mistaken him for somebody else, Kevin smiles and dives his hands into his pockets and searches desperately! why is this happening with him? He has his new image, he has his new life why is the security guard searching him?

"I'm sorry I've left it in the changing rooms I must have left it there "

He says still smiling

"Well you won't mind if we going to check then son will you "

The brute demands

Kevin looks annoyed! I mean what was any different with him and any other customer how dare this steroid monster invade his personal space, not when he was spending good earned cash, well good stolen cash anyways.

Kevin says in his posh voice

"Actually, yes I do mind I'm a paying customer I have bought these goods and I wish to leave"

as he says this, the monkey like security guard grabs him by the shoulder and begins to drag him backwards Kevin is no match for this monster. The monster drags him back to the cubicle he got changed in and throws him in face first. As Kevin lands he smacks his upper lip and he immediately tastes blood. He pushes his hand down to get his receipt to find there is about one thousands of them scrunched up, mixed in with all sorts of other junk, he desperately starts searching through the pile while the beast breathes like a velociraptor, intensely staring at behind him from behind. After about ten mins of searching the security guard loses his patience and pulls Kevin to his feet and stuffs his hand in to kevs pocket, drags out his wad of cash and pulls a big part of it off, then slams Kevin back to the ground

"next time pay for your shit, fuckin junkie cunt "

He says, in disgust

"now get the fuck out my store "

He now says as if he is not a security guard, as if he is the owner of all Primark's, and this was some rich persons undercover tv show where he pretends to be a security guard for the day

Kevin wants to argue back and reclaim his money, but he is running out of fight, he looks at him in disgust stands to his feet and shuffles sadly away to the front doors of the store. This wasn't shaping up to be a very good start at all, He leaves the store at least he had his new clothes. He walks up a hill towards more shops and he sees a small café called

MRS SNOWS CAFE

He starts to walk towards it in the hope of a nice pick me up and also maybe a chance of job. as he approaches the shop an old woman comes to greet him at the glass door, he smiles at her. what a nice little shop, he thinks, she's even getting the door for him, what courtesy. Suddenly the sound of rejection slams into Kevin's life again, she snaps the lock shut on the door and turns the sign to closed and the woman doesn't even give him the respect of looking at him. He feels a deep mix of rage and disappointment, I mean this was meant to be his human paradise but instead was shaping up to be just as bad a nightmare as his previous home. Surely there must be a place for him in this world, surely his human temptation and misery couldn't follow him everywhere. He thinks about getting a bottle of cheap vodka and giving up, this surely can't be the only way out. There must be another way, he walks on towards another local shop. In the window his eyes scan, and they see the very thing he was trying to avoid, a gleaming bottle of clear liquid, the front label stating Rachmaninov vodka. He shakes his head and dismisses the image from his mind, carrying on in disgust. No, he will not be beaten! He has the urge to change, this surely must still be enough. He carries on towards the end of a street there is a William hill bookmakers where three skinny teenage kids are standing talking to each other , one of the three has a thin black bomber jacket and blonde hair he's smoking a cigarette and bellowing the exhaled poison out in to the world, the other one also skinny with a dark blonde beard wearing a woven dark green jumper with dark blue jeans, the last teenager fully dressed in black his jacket covered in a yellow compass design. As soon as Kevin starts to walk towards the group the blonde haired one nudges the black coated one and then they all take notice of him, as soon as they do this Kevin realises they have and begins to look down at the ground, In an attempt to pass by unnoticed, this was not going to be the case as Kevin begins to get closer the group descends on him.

"alright were you heading mate "

The black clothed one says, getting right into his face, speaking like they had known each other for years, as soon as kevs goes to answer he notices the bearded teen has started acting as a lookout. The blonde hair one rushes right tight up against Kevin and looks straight in his eyes

"you got any fucking cash mate "

Once again as Kevin goes to answer he rams his hand in to kevs pocket and rips out all the cash. He doesn't even count it, he just slides it into his back pocket

"please no don't "

Kevs said quietly. As he does the black dressed one smashes his fist into to Kevin's face and as it draws back, Kevin realises through the pain, he has been hit by a sovereign ring with around penny attached to it is golden shanks, for some reason he focuses on this ring while this horror unfolds, Kevin can only stare at the ring. He had seen them before in the window of Argos, sovereign rings everyone was wearing them just now. As he is contemplating the rings, the blonde one raises his knees in a kickboxing manner in to kevs stomach and blood spatters out of his mouth. A pain spreads across his abdomen and his vision goes yellow zig zag, colours fade, and his vision moves back into reality. He receives four more hits to the face then after the zig zag haze clears again, he is staring at t their feet, there is no remembrance of him falling down, there are several kicks to him while he's on the ground. They decide that's enough and start moving off laughing, as Kevin looks up there splitting his money between the three. A tear rolls down kevs face and mixes with the blood, he stares in sadness at his own blood spattered in front of him, after several minutes he manages to get himself to his feet.

Kevin wipes his hand across his face and removes the blood and mud and wipes it on his leg. He trembles back along the road to the shop he had passed earlier and click the door opens and an, antique stile bell bings and Kevin walks in ....

Chapter 16 the crossover

Coopers eyes are about to close forever, when he hears something that's different, something that's not the noise of passing bugs or rats chewing at his box, even they scurry fast when they get a whiff of him, never close enough for him to feed on. This was a different noise altogether it wasn't nature, it wasn't animal, IT WAS HUMAN. For the first time in century's Cooper had hope, this eternal nightmare could end. His eyes moving around in his now, stone body tries to look backwards, and his stone ears listen intensely. What is it? He thinks, in his cloudy mind, then it gets a bit louder. Its shouting, angry shouting, well ok that's a good sign, whoever this is is pissed off and likely to stumble upon Cooper by accident or even alert others to him. Coopers intelligence was diminishing and drifting from the status of village idiot in to cave man intelligence as the petrification spreads in to his brain. He moves his eyes down towards to inspect his body nothing but pure darkness an abyss of nothingness, He pictures his body in its perfect state, the way it was the day he drank from his last beautiful victim. Suddenly he starts to hear sobbing and crying, he looks backwards again then the first real sound he's heard in years, a massive crash then a smash, then suddenly something he couldn't possible expected after five hundred years. His box is illuminated with light, oh my god! He is being exhumed, a thousand possibilities now float about his stone like mind. He was going to play it safe, wait till he was alone with some historian and use all his ability to bite his hand and refuel his body and break free of this torture. Ahhh at last, he will be free. He turns his eyes back down to his body, horrific terror fills the perfect vision he has of his body. There is no perfect body, water from the fall has made it into his box and its trickling along to his head. His body is dissolving one piece at a time, his arms and legs flaking like shredded wheat, his cheek half gone. He looks intensely at his cheek, a piece slides off like a piece of fish scale, it lands on the water flow and drifts off like a boat and out of a small hole. He sits analysing his body further then it changes the sobbing and crying then he hears some words he doesn't hear all of as the muddy water and wooden box muffle the sounds,

"IM SIC- OF -YOU-A—TH-S IS THE E—FU-K ALL OF Y—I M CH—KIN-OUT"

Things go quiet then, a scent flows into his nose, a torturous smell, blood, human blood. Involuntary his eyes pin towards the smell and turn red, this was like further punishment for Cooper to be so close to what he needs but not able to get it. Whoever was out there was dying, they must be bleeding out, what was all this about? What had happened in five hundred years? Then a sound he didn't expect laughing, the evillest laugh he has ever heard, except his own. What the fuck is happening? A stranger has arrived on a walk into the wilderness and banged his head, it poured outs with blood and then reawakens and started laughing in a crooked way. I mean what is happening the laugh gets more and more distant

"Noooooo"

 he's leaving, that is a bad scenario, so close but so far!

"comeee back"

 copper shouts in his mind

"I need your blood "

His mind now screams

It all goes silent, that was his only chance gone, this was truly the end for Cooper, a legend finished forever. There would be no more talk, no more him, he thought. That's sad. He closes his eyes and they slowly begin to turn in to stone and his thoughts become more and more silent, more and more distant, the end is finally here.

He thinks one last time, he feels a bit of his face crack and slide off and move away from him into the flowing water of his casket, he was going to melt, no more Cooper just a pile of stone and dust

Goodbye Copper!

As Kevin enters the shop his blood-filled nose is met by a dusky old smell, the mix of newspapers and old fruit combined with the millions of others little nick knacks scattered around, he turns his immediate attention to the bottle of vodka he had seen earlier.

The shop keeper who is probably "Mr Aziz" as it said over the shop on entry is looking very concerned by Kevin, he is covered in bruises cuts and blood and looks quite disturbing to the general public

"can I help you "

He says reluctantly

Kevin peels through the pain in his ribs and sides and utters words

"yes, can I have one litre of Rachmaninov and twenty regal king-size "

The man looks at him intensely and doesn't even reach for the products

"that will be fifteen-pound thirty-six please "

Kevin sighs and takes off his shoe and in it is two twenty-pound notes and ten, the only good thing he always done religiously is always put a bit of his money in to his shoe. He pulls out the twenty pound note and gives it to the shop keeper who instantly looks relived, the shop keeper turns round to get the vodka and cigarettes while Kevin puts his thirty pound back in to his shoe and puts it on the shop keeper rings up his till and takes out the change and hands it to Kevin he looks at it "one more thing please "

He says the shop keeper shrugs at him

"Wilkeston razor blades "

The shop keeper looks him up and down and the points him to a stand filled with little bags, Kevin scowls intensely knitting needles, buttons, toe separators and yes razor blades. He takes a packet and returns to the counter

"ninety-nine pence please "

The shop keeper says without any expression. Kevin hand him a pound coin from his change and then throws it in to the bag along with the cigarettes and alcohol. He then heads out the shop, peers round and sees nothing that catches his attention. Kevin looks at the corner street sign one picket reads, bus station, he doesn't show any joy or expression merely just starts walking in that direction, en route he passes many people who all have a good look at his injuries and talk behind their hands about him,

He has no interest in any of them as he cannot even face them, anymore, he finally reaches the bus station and he looks up, to a large illuminated board and scrolls down with his eyes 11:01 to Glencoe arriving 13:28. He goes to a small window at the rear of the train station encased in a concrete wall a small glowing sign above it stating

TICKETS

 Kevin looks at in no interest he approaches the window.

"one ticket to Glencoe "

He doesn't even look at the worker

"you can say please you know "

She blurts

He looks up he is met by a middle-aged woman with short red hair and pointed glasses, he sighs and looks at the price behind her. Nine pound eighty, he takes his tenner from shoe and throws it in to the window, the woman looks at him in disgust for a few seconds then begins to print his ticket, Kevin snatches it moves away from the window and looks for his bus. It doesn't take long he sees the busses all stacked like dominos. He goes to walk to his bus and trips over a kerb and falls flat on his face the whole bus station ignites with laughter, not one person comes to his aid he pulls himself to his feet doesn't look at anyone and heads towards the bus labelled Glencoe. He goes on the bus, the driver is looking at him while trying not to snigger about his fall, Kevin holds back his tears further than he has already been doing, the driver ushers him on the bus Kevin moves to the back of the bus, the bus driver sighs and laughs again , Kevin ignores him and moves right to the last seat and lays his bag down. He lays on top of it, pulls his jacket over his head starts to quietly cry and go to sleep, in his subconscious, he hears the bus ignite. And drifts awake for a minute as somebody has sat down beside him. Uggghhh, what now, who was going to give him shit now, he pulls his jacket down.

He must rub his eyes a Second & third time to see what he sees

"ddd…. dad "

His father sitting there sure as the day

"dad I thought you were in jail "

His dad smiles back at him

"I am son this isn't real "

Tears slide down poor Kevin's face, he rubs his eyes intensely while crying into his hands, why? He thinks he looks back up his father still there, staring at him

He talks again

"real or not my boy you need to listen, you're making a big mistake. Choose a different route, there's always a way to improve life and there's always someone to help "

Kevin looks at him from a more agitated angle now in almost disbelief.

"DAD I'm a junkie, alcoholic, broke, friendless, girlfriendless, homeless, beaten, unemployable, wanted by police, and let's be honest probably fucking dying!! what do I need to do for a break around here? You were never any fuckin use, all you fuckers just abandoned me my whole life what other way could I have gone "

His dad looks down to the ground in sadness   and then looks back at him

"no matter what happens now son"

"I love you "

Kevin puts his hand over his eyes as the words cut him like a knife, he looks up to tell his dad he loves him too, but like his luck his dad has vanished as ,well that just the way life was going, he thought and returned to his jacket of tears.

The bus rumbled and squeaked for the next few hours, his mind kept moving back and forth from reality. Each time it gets closer to oblivion just for a brief moment, it stopped being sore in his head, he forgot all the sadness and pain and it all swept away, but in seconds it would all come flooding back and melt in to his conscious, forcing him back in the deeper realm of his mind. Eventually the pace of the vehicle slowed to a complete stop he felt all his internal organs pull against gravity then re-centre. He peered over his hood like a scared meercat, his field of vision met by people disembarking and reaching above their seats for jackets and bags, he pulls his body left and right until the pins and needles pass then he pulls his sorry ass to its feet, stretches and gives a final left and right turn to clear the pins and needles. He shuffles along the bus like a broken robot and passes the cocky driver who still gives a sniggered look at him, Kevin doesn't even care now he walks off. He is met by landscapes of beautiful greens and browns all melting in to a large-scale vista of nature's perfection, the scene cut across the middle by a razor-sharp horizon of grey clouds, the occasional bursts of glowing yellow sunshine sending rays of beauty on to the landscape like the hand of god. Kevin moves off the bus his feet are met by gravel mixed in with soft mud, he struggles away from the bus leaving it more and more shrinking in to the vista to a point till it is barely visible, even in his depressed state he look round and is astonished by the beauty of this place. There is barley any people here, it is untouched by humanity, this is a good thing Kevin thinks. He searches long and hard for the perfect place, there are so many here to choose but he wants the perfect one. Suddenly he finds an opening over a small stone bridge, as he enters the opening there is a large swirling pool of crystal-clear water, so clear that he can see all the way to the bottom. He can make out individual rocks and see dark spots where the bed of this watery lake disappears into small caves, there is a small waterfall running down into the lake and a very clear field of mist emanating from it.

This is it, Kevin thinks, what a beautiful place, he turns the final corner to see the end result, NO! what is he met by NO! what are the chance two backpackers, both with matching green and pink hiking sticks. They appear to be ruining Kevin's special spot by sitting down, enjoying a sandwich and cup of coffee. Kevin freeze frames the world in the hope they would just vanish, he stares at them and they also take notice of him for a few minutes they are locked into an ultimate staring match, Kevin sighs and turns back and leaves. What where the chances? He carries back out of the opening and along a long winding road he comes to a side road. onwards states A828 ahead of him, to the left the B3608, he chooses the latter, in the hope that there will be no way there will be anyone to bump in to.

He walks what seems like years along thin ascending and long tracks and round bending corners. He sees a large opening in a stone wall worn away with time, intrigued he walks toward it and peers in, there is a large walkway overgrown and built of interwind rose and raspberry bushes. He thinks to himself this is the perfect place to escape to, no one will be down here. He forces his way in carefully round all the bushes avoiding them carefully. He starts to see a clearing ahead of the bushes, he pushes through, suddenly his eyes are met by an array of natural beauty and disbelief.

There is a slim waterfall, it slides down the perfect natural cut gorge. Rocks rise then break in the middle like massive stone pancakes that have been unevenly stacked up then fallen over with time, smashing Down in to the ground and somehow merging in to the ground in a unique way like they have always been there. To the left of the fall, a glowing purple field of brilliance as the purple shades of the Scottish heather melts in to the under-growth root and grass. At the bottom of the water fall it spills in to a zig zag stream, colliding past the year-old debris of rocks that have fallen from the triangular cliff tops above, the water now running as clear and clean as the air surrounding the stream. Rocks varying in size all cracked like circuitry and large patches of dark green moss, emphasizing from corners and gaps like infection. Nature at its best. To stand back and look at the whole scene from afar, the effect of liquid clouds running down a mountain can be a fair assessment. There is a tear that runs down Kevin's face. He has found his place. He gives the glen one finale last look for unwanted hikers or any other un wanted human's, nothing! this place was all his place no interruption, finally a place to Die, to finally be free of the pain no more failing no more judgment it was all coming to a finally! The great life of Kevin is about to come to closure, he gives a sigh of relief and moves towards the waterfall, he sits down on a rock and closes his eyes then pulls out a cigarette and lights it "well no point in hanging around"

He mutters to himself

He rips the lid off his vodka and takes an almighty swig, the ice-cold fire burns down his throat and settles badly into his stomach. All his aches and pains seem to numb a little, he touches his ribs. nope still there, he takes another almighty swig and the pain subsides quicker. He repeats this process on and off for about an hour till there is only a quarter left in the bottle, and not much left in the respect of fear or common sense. Kevin reaches in to the bag and pulls out the razor blades, tears were now fully streaming down Kevin's face

He stands to his feet and screams at the top of his voice

"IM SICK OF YOU ALL!! THIS IS THE END FUCK ALL OF YOU I M CHECKIN OUT"

He runs one of the razor blades across his wrist the pain is still intense even though Kevin has drunk so much, he looks at his wrist, expecting a Jason horror scene but there is little blood, just a small trickle running sideways off his wrist he looks with disbelief

"god I can't even kill myself right"

He takes the blade and cuts deeper in to his other wrist this time an array of blood spatters all over the vista slowly funnelling down leaves and rocks, Kevin falls to his knees he now looks back at his other wrist to see blood pouring from it as well he begins to lose the power in his body he lies down at the edge of the stream so he can see the waterfall. His hands begin to turn cold and spread up his arms, his neck now loses power and his head falls in to the stream sideways, half his head in and out, he opens his mouth and gasps for air, but all strength has gone, at last the pain was fading, he was almost complete, almost free of this hell on earth. The eye in the water was blacked out now, his open eye focuses on something in the stream moving towards him, a large grey piece of what looks like rock. It is moving closer to his head, what is it this thing? Kevin tries to move away from it but he was completely paralysed, at the end of his life, bloodless and dying. His eye, all bloodshot from the fear of suicide and this mysterious floating rock heading towards him, focuses on it as it moves towards his mouth, as it gets closer he is able to make it out a little better , a little fleck of what looks like graphite but on it, what looks like tiny little strands of fine string worms, wriggling in every direction. He tries to summon the strength to avoid this strange object, but it slides in his mouth. Suddenly there was no longer a calm feeling of pain free reality, his throat reactivates all the nerves to feel a thousand needles pinpointing into his head, torso, arms and legs. He blacks in and out of consciousness each time, screaming in agony, writhing around the ground like he's on fire. He screams echoing round the glen and birds fly away from trees as he does finally, he pulls himself to his feet and tries to figure out what's happening. Is he dead? No, there's no pain in death, or so he heard, he cannot focus, waves and waves of pain are pouring over his entire being as he bursts out of the glen screaming and running. He makes it to the road that had led him in there, dark now he stumbles down it trying to reach the main road in hope of an ambulance. He must have ingested some kind of poison, he doesn't know why he's not died yet from slashing his wrists, but anything would be better than this pain. He's nearly at the bottom of the windy street where he had left the main route when something strange happens, his heart thudding in his chest, so hard slows down dramatically, he feels his chest,

"oh, my fuckin god my hearts have has stopped "

He screams in a panic and falls backwards, suddenly all the pain stops, he must be dying now. Confusion, fills Kevin, his pupils suddenly tighten, and his vision sharpens to a level he can't explain, looking around him the whole world has become high definition, all the small parts of the world illuminated. He looks at his wrist and falls back in shock, the wounds are healed, gone, repaired, then the pain moves down from his eyes and like a draining sink starts flowing down his body till it was gone altogether. What the hell was happening, Kevin looks at his skin it was lighter, clean and free of all smoke, drink, drugs, anything that had given it that dirty tinge. He feels his ribs and various other points of injury, to the points of where the pain had been, nothing it had all left. Now a power of euphoria flew up his entire body, wow, it feels like the first time he had ever taken drugs but times six hundred. He screams in power and jumps forward, to his astonishment he leaps about six metres forward and lands firmly on his feet, he leans back on a wall, behind him and instead of the concreate giving him stability his hand smashes through it in an effortless move. He whips round and looks at the wall something has changed his power it was unreal. Had he ingested some super plant or alien meteor. a million theories fill Kevin head, he starts to walk slowly, bit by bit, getting more control over his new speed and strength. It doesn't take long it surprises him, he was always slow at picking things up but it's like his brain is running a million miles an hour. After walking down in the dark, he starts to see the first place he had gone to kill himself first, suddenly a rage fills him he punches another stone on the top of a wall, it evaporates in to dust.

"those cunts, hill walking, goody two shoes fucks, how dare they fuck with my plans they are going to suffer "

These two hill walkers had been the last two people to piss of Kevin and push him to the edge. He looks in the place he had last seen the walkers there, is no one there in their place, a glowing orange tent illuminated by a yellow light. Kevin smiles, thinks about scaring them using his new strength to throw big stones towards their tent but then something weird happens, a hunger flows over Kevin and instead of it being for food or water all he can picture is the inside of one of the walkers, he had never even seen their insides but all human insides he had ever seen or thought about where a pulsing water fountain of fresh human blood like a butchers window. No rocks, weren't enough to fix this, they must pay all of them, everyone who lead to this unfair life of his. He was going to serve up every one of them and show them the true meaning of suffering, and finally Kevin will have the power, the strength to do it. Was a this all a dream? Kevin didn't care he was going to enjoy this immensely. He walks over towards the tent but before he even gets close, he realises he can here every word they are saying without being that near, he stands close and waits for his chance ...

Chapter 18 Kevin's revenge

Paul and jo were a couple of love, a couple of excitement, they had been travelling the world in their early twenties, fell in love and got married on the French alps, right in front of the famous Chamonix mountain range of the alps. They loved exploring but were desperate to go home and start a family, they had seen enough for now Thailand, brazil, Mexico, Grand Canyon, and many more but one thing was left to hike, the beautiful Scottish Highlands and islands dream of both of them. This will be one last thing to do, then they can settle. So they got their best tent and their matching hiking sticks, they got as a wedding present and headed for Scotland. Their first stop, Edinburgh for a day, then hire a car, then the drive and ramble of the famous and stunning Glencoe. The perfect way to end their world ramblings ...

Paul looks over at jo, she is brushing her hair into a small camping mirror, he smiles. Wow, I love that girl, he thinks to himself. he stands up from his knees in the tent and stretches.

"I'm going to head out and clean my cup in the lake "

He puts forward towards her, she looks up and nods in agreeance. He then moves out the tent and leaves jo to her hair brushing that she seem content doing .

As Kevin sits waiting patiently in a shroud of close bushes, he cannot feel his heartbeat anymore but now another heart beat pulsing below a warm chest. He looks over at the tent as one of the walkers was emerging, he move's over to the calm clean water and begin rinsing out some kind of cup.

What to do now? A razor-sharp plan fills his mind, no more uncertainty, no more fear or doubt. Kevin takes in a deep breath and smells an intense familiar scent ...urine ...pish ... the walker is urinating into the lake, rage fills his eyes, he moves in in a flash, within a second he is standing behind him. The walker, Paul, hasn't even noticed, he's whistling as he pees. No, no this will not do Kevin thinks! he grabs him and jumps with all his new strength at an unhuman rate over to the other side of the lake, this happens so fast that the only noise at the urinating site would have been a quick puff of air. Paul never even had a chance to yelp

Paul is in shock as Kevin drops him to the ground in front of him, Paul shakes for a minute and turns over to see what had lifted him, he looks surprised he was expecting to see a large hawk or griffin instead to find little Kevin

"Wwwwhat happened? who are you? "

He mutters out in fear

"DON'T YOU REMEMBER ME I LOOKED IN HERE ONLY A MATTER OF HOURS AGO"

Kevin says firmly and quickly awaiting answer

Paul looks confused and looks at him closer

"I'm sorry I never noticed you "

He says reluctantly hopping Kevin has the wrong person.

"YOU NNNN!"

"YOU NEVER N!"

"YOU NEVER FUCKKKING NOTICED ME THAT'S THE PROBLEM! NO ONE FUCKING NOTICES ME !!!!!!!"

As Kevin screams this he grabs Pauls arm tearing it clean off his body and throws it in to the lake. Blood spatters across Kevin's face, he gives out an evil smile as Paul rolls in pain not even screaming, just in complete terror and shock. He crouches down beside Paul who is whimpering, trying to say jo's name but Kevin grabs his face and squeezes, his face pulps in to a jellified mess, there is an open hole in his face now and a dark cocktail of blood is just pouring from it. Pauls lifeless body falls flat to the ground, Kevin's new super hearing detects a noise from across the lake

"Paul are you there …it's not funny Paul come out NOW"

Kevin jumps in two motions back to the tent site landing completely in front of jo

"hello"

Kevin says calmly

"ahhhhhhhhhhhhhhhhh PAUL "

Jo screams at the fullest of her voice, Kevin lets out his evil smile again, looks her up and down, she is wearing a tee-shirt tight against her small breasts, no fabric between her upper tummy and pant line and black panties with a ninja on them. Should he rape her? Kevin thinks, he puts this to his new brain, as he had never been that successful with the ladies his mind comes back negative, he seems to have lost all sexual attraction or urge instead he punches her in the jaw breaking it instantly. she falls to the ground with the force of a falling piano. As she tries to talk, blood spurts from her mouth, tears flow from her face soaking the ground. Suddenly he feels his eyes sharpen and pin point on his victim, his jawline begins to rumble, he feels his teeth, two pointed teeth have emerged from his upper gum just in front of his normal teeth. He kneels beside jo she is shaking in terror and fear. He thinks to himself shall he drink from her neck? no that's far too Hollywood, whatever he had become this was legend, not fantasy thought up in some studio by pricks. He smashes his jaw into her back, biting at the same time, she screams intensely filling the whole region with her last fears of this life. A chunk is removed from her back the size of a dinner plate, Kevin spits it to one side as the hole in her back starts to pool with blood he rams his face in to it and drains the sweet warm blood, it runs into his body like a balloon expanding inside a tube and implodes with power like Kevin has never known pure bliss, the best feeling he has ever felt. He rips his face out of the twitching, now dead, jo and screams into the air. His new incisors glowing pearly white in the moonlight. He sits back and enjoys this for a long while lying next to the dead jo and listening to the nature around him. He pulls himself to his feet and now he will get his revenge on them all, in order of the ways they treated him, first the sniggering bus driver

He dips his finger in jo's back and writes on a stone wall and laughs

RIP PAUL AND JO.

Chapter 19 Harrys Bus

Harry stood surrounded by all his friends at the end of the bar, a complete array of people from a middle-aged woman, to a tall muscular man with a pointed moustache. Just past him, a thin skinny chap who looks barely alive, like all the alcohol had rotted away every part of his body, they all stand and sit listening carefully to Harrys story, the story probably wasn't that interesting but harry was a pub man. He lived for his alcohol, lived for the social dependence of the pub environment. He had always drunk his whole life since he can remember so this was his only way. He stands in his bright pink golf jumper and finishes his story

"And so that was it, Ker splat! The wee fucker went down like a brick but no just that, in front of everybody in the whole station! "

He then patted a couple of people on the back while laughing to encourage there laughing, they all follow suit and ignite in laughter...

"Ahh you should have seen it, ha-ha don't think we will ever see that wee prick ever again, he was headed into nowhere "

He looks down for a second almost like he was praying for Kevin but almost immediately his attention back to the small blonde barmaid

"Hey honey, can I get a wee half and a nip please? "

He puts his full charm on here forgetting he's an overweight, almost bald, middle aged bus driver. In his head he believes that he is still the beauty of his seventeen -year-old self, but the true reality has been blinded for him with years of his practiced routine .The barmaid doesn't even give him the time of day, she shrewdly smirks at him and drops the smirk in a split second. The bar maid begins to start pouring his beer and whisky, he keeps smiling at her like he has won her heart. This process continues for many hours as one by one the people round him leave and go home. Eventually when he realises that the only person left is old Scott, a withered shaken man that we spoke of earlier. Harry realises that he is looking at a horror reflection of his own future, but it was too late to go back and he was too self-deluded to care. There was no chance that there was any change going to happen in his life soon! So, he pulls himself to his feet and leaves the pub, the barmaid looks relived as he leaves knowing that she will not have to repel his sexual advances and arse feeling as she ushers him out at closing time! He pushes through the full-length double doors and the air hits him like a ton of bricks, his lungs filling with cool, Inverness air, as opposed to the nice warm beer smelling air that his lungs had been enjoying for the last good few hours. He pulled his jacket tight up to his neck and turned his whole-body round and looked at the pub to see his glorious sanctuary

THE COCKREL AND SLIPPER

Like his drinking status for the night, the lights went out and the pub suddenly looked like a derelict building. A million grandiose plans go through Harrys head, strip bars where stripper's rub there small nineteen-year-old year-old breasts and clits in his face? Or, Night clubs where smoke machine's cast lasers in the open night while he pours sambuca into his mouth ,setting it on fire. Even a lively piano bar would do, anything but the harsh reality, the little but nowhere scenario he faces! As these plans are formalising, they must now end, Harry was an act, nothing more than to please on his own ego! The harsh reality hits hard, as he reaches his front door and is met by overgrown hedges and uneven slabs, the ground beneath them pushing weeds out like alien invaders. His front door worn, red paint untouched by maintenance for decades, why paint? When that money could be spent in the pub Harry has always thought. He reaches in to his pocket it is soaked by a mixture of sweat and urine from not shacking properly while in the men's room. Eventually in this moist pocket of dust and piss, he finds his single key attached to a bus key. After two or three attempts he gets it in the lock, and he turns it and enters. He forces past a pile of bills unopened on the floor behind the door and tramples along his hall until getting to the midway light switch, igniting this hardly even makes a difference for him, the light bulb is 40w, it was a cheap deal at the corner shop. Harry thought a penny saved equals one more whisky. He continues down his very poorly maintained hall, socks and rubbish lying everywhere, finally reaching a couch thin and worn, light green shade in colour! He planks down in a drunken force, the couch jangles with empty bottles. He stuffs his hand down the side of the sofa and pulls out a dusty old remote and turns on a small television that has a coat hanger as an ariel. He flicks on to channel four and there is a movie just starting he smiles in excitement!

 TITANIC

Excellent he thinks what a way to end this perfect evening, he pulls over to the other side of the couch to reveal a bottle of famous grouse whisky and a dirty little tumbler. He pours a whisky and drinks it in one, the film begins he tries to focus on it as he drinks several more shots of whisky in succession

"that Kate Winslet would fucking get it, wee slut "

He mutters to himself

he unfastens his trousers in the notion of relieving himself in a violent wank over Kate Winslet. When he passes out, penis in hand, the glass falls in front of him and smashes into tiny pieces this wasn't enough to wake up poor Harry, he was gone for the night!...

Buuuuuuuuuuuzzzzzzzzzzzzzzzzzzzzzzzzzz

Buuuuuuuuuuuuuzzzzzzzzzzzzzzzzzzzzzz

Harry wakes into a noise of irritation, he sits up barely even to function, he throws his shoe at the alarm clock it stops buzzing immediately. His brain switching on each function one at a time like a giant space craft being powered up, first traction to rise him to a sitting position the toe's wriggling, a surge of power to the eye, opening pinpoint pupils bloodshot. He fastens up his trousers and stands to his feet like a zombie, he moves in to his bathroom and stands in front of toilet undos his fly and begins to urinate. For the next ten minutes he continues to urinate the smell of urine and reconstituted booze flowing up to his nostrils. Normally for most human being this would be disgusting and bring them to sickness but not harry, this was the norm. After his enormous pee he drops his clothes off like a snake skin and pushes them to one side with his foot and starts a shower, almost immediately he feels a twinge in his lower bowel, he turns round and sits down on the very dirty toilet and within one minute of awkward twitches and pushes he's done, he doesn't even wipe just pours himself a shot of Listerine and starts to swirl it round his mouth and enters the shower. The water at his feet turns yellow, he pours half a bottle of shampoo over his head and lets it run down his whole body, once he gets out, he dries off with an already damp towel. He then pulls from the top of a laundry basket a pair of black trousers and a sweater with COACH-GO written on it. He leaves and heads for the bus station. You see harry is a working alcoholic, and like any working alcoholic they can never admit it. They believe if they are working a full day, they are safe from all the down sides of being an alcoholic and somewhat invincible. He walks down with the cold air bouncing off his face, still the alcohol in his blood stream combating it like an energy shield, finally after three streets he reaches the Inverness bus station

"morning harry "

A plump red-faced gentleman says as he enters the courtyard, Harry waves back with a smile on his face

Words were never very high at this time of the morning, he felt a wave would suffice, he looks at the big blue coach with the large letters on it GLENCOE and sighs, here we go again. He thinks he remembers a film he had seen recently were a man was reporting on a groundhog and time kept repeating every day, that was Harrys life a rerun of some sad working alcoholic who can't change. He entered the bus using his key the doors de pressurised and open, he sits down and adjusts all his mirrors and waits twenty-seven minutes, after that he could then disembark, in this period about eight people enter his bus two middle aged hill walkers one , a   large fat man and the rest just to unimportant to remember. At last he could start this course of events that would lead him back to the pub with each and every journey he got closer to his pub life, one started, three to go he thought. He starts the almighty engine it erupts like a pack of passing boars, he pulls away and heads off but little does he know this is the last time he will ever have to suffer this journey, little does he know this will be the last time he suffers anything!

Kevin sits thinking about the order in how he was going to make them all pay, this wasn't going to be another fuck up! This was going to be the perfect plan. He knew what time to get his victims, he knew where they would be, well most of them anyway, they would all suffer to the same level of humiliation and pain he had felt. He sits waiting patiently against a moss covered rockface using his new eyes to analyse everything, a simple leaf is no longer just a leaf it's an intricate city of tightly packed streets and houses all weaved in to the veins of this beautiful creation. As he's analysing this he hears a engine approach, his eyes look up over the rim of the rock and his eyes turn from colour to complete black, his mouth sharpens, black veins pulsate on his face in a shimmer. He focuses on the cab of the bus, yes it was him, the sniggering bus driver.

"thought it was funny did you !!!!!"

"well the laughs on you, fat bus driving cunt"

Kevin mutters under his breath

He tightens his new fangs together and gets ready to pounce. Kill everything near the bus in some horrific scene of violence. No wait, that would be silly, that would have consequences, now this was a strange concept for Kevin normally he would jump in to things without much thought, his mind clouded, but now it was all clear he knew exactly what to do. He scraps the first plan, no murder, no mayhem, just takes it slow and calculated. He sits twitching in anticipation as the occupants of the bus disembark one by one. They all leave and head off in their own direction he notices one of them is very overweight man wearing kilt and a pink scarf, weird, he thinks but dismisses it quickly. He waits and waits for his chance and its come, the driver moves to the back of the bus and has undone his trousers and starts to urinate while yawning, this was his chance he uses all his new speed and swishes onto the bus in a flash, he quickly looks at the named bag in the cab of the bus .

"HARRY"

He smiles and goes to the back of the bus and slides down out of view while still smiling, harry now re-enters the bus and waits for the time to pass, no one enters, it was very rare for Harry to get a passenger back on the morning run. He looks up and down the bus and sets off, he really should check every seat for lost possessions and sometimes he did but today he just wanted to get back to the pub. He drives a steady pace, bit by bit, turning the weaving Glencoe roads he gets to point where it starts to climb up high into the hills, this was the bit in-between Glencoe and fort William. Suddenly there is a bang from inside the bus, he slows, what the hell was that? That never happens. He tries to look round but there is no way to concentrate on the road and check, had something fallen off the bus? he must investigate, these roads are dangerous enough without debris on the road. He sees a parking/passing point up ahead, he pulls in and shuts the engine down, disembarks and starts walking round the bus.

"nothing "

He mutters

What the hell could it have been he thinks? Oh well back on the road one step closer to the pub, he sits back in his seat and is about to set off but wait, what is it, something is different, something is out of place. He turns around slowly and to his horror he has a passenger, white fear fills his body. How could this have happened? Had he missed him getting on in Glencoe? No he checked the bus. He could have never got on away up here, Harry moves a couple of rows toward the strange passenger. As he stares at harry with black seductive eyes of mystery and unknown reason.

"hello c.c.an I help you son"

He says in a broken nervous way

Nothing, no reply, no noise just the stare. As he gets closer, he sees that it is the young boy who tripped in the station, phew, that wee dweeb he thinks.

"how did you get on? Did you get on in Glencoe "?

"Answer me son or I'll drag your wee skinny ass off here and leave you in the middle of nowhere "

Kevin stands and takes three steps forward, shadow and bad lighting distort his face

"Right that's it off with you, I got a schedule to keep"

Harry says in an angry tone

 This little prick is interfering with his drinking schedule, that could not be allowed he grabs kevs arm and goes to pull him, Kevin doesn't even budge he is like a concrete block, nothing had the power to move , Harry looks confused as he tugs at him. Kevin just keeps smiling, Harry now looks concerned but before he has any more time to worry, Kevin single slaps the side of his head instantly rendering him unconscious. A haze of darkness instantly fills Harry's eyes, a burst of zigzag yellow into his vision like tunnels with a single white dot in the middle. Then nothing, utter oblivion, empty universe, no thought, no sound, no reality a tight packed pocket that not even time and space could enter. There is an orange flash in the void of darkness, then another, his eyes begin to open, the world is the wrong, nothing is the way it should be. He turns his head hoping he is just still waking out of this daze, but NO! He is upside down hanging off a precipice, hundreds of metres above the ground. He looks back down the to drop now underneath him, there are small sheep and a stream, they look like an oil painting because they are so far away. He pulls all muscle in his fat flab to look up and see what's holding his legs. To his absolute terror he sees Kevin sitting quite calmly holding one if his legs still smiling.

"good morning Harry I've been hanging around for you "

Kevin lets out an evil laugh and goes back to him smiling

"Suddenly Harry realises something we all fear, he's going to die! A cold dark fuzz fills his brain and he realises he is unable to stop shivering, a feeling of disbelief, primatal alert system is now active in his brain"

"please I have done nothing to you, I don't want to die "

He says in between sobs, Kevin looks at him and pulls him up so they're almost face to face

"you all did something "

He says quietly in Harrys ear, with this he pushes his index finger into Harrys abdomen and it goes in like soft butter harry tries to breathe but blood trickles out his mouth.

"Heeelllp"

Blood splutters as he tries to form words, now Kevin begins to swing him like a clock pendulum, each time on return he batters him off the pointed rock of the cliff edge and each time shredding more and more skin and bone. Each time harry moves back in and out of painful consciousness the pain sends him back quick. He finally   wakes up in his seat in the cabin of his bus , the seat belt fully extended and wrapped around him holding him in place he now shuffles desperately trying to move. He looks out the window and Kevin is standing there smiling. he waves, harry notices the bus is now pointing towards the cliff edge

"when somebody falls the thing to do is laugh, Harry! Is that not right! "

Kevin screams at him now in an angry tone

Harry whispers

"Sorry"

Kevin moves to the back of the bus and without much effort pushes the full weight of the coach towards the edge. Harrys eyes enlarge as the coach begins to tip, he thinks back at how his life had been such a waste.

Dedicating his life to a poison, consumed by overgrown monkeys, a way of life where everybody is selfish and only interested in remaining in booze. The coach begins to tip Harry's eyes flood with tears, the coach falls like a milk carton.

It lands sideways on to a stone ledge pancaking in to a fire ball of smoke Kevin looks down at the burning mess and sniggers in a sarcastic way.

"so sorry Harry looks like I missed the bus "

A loud evil laugh fills the morning air

Kevin turns and looks at the empty road in front of him, hmm I wonder how quick I can run to inverness he thinks? ......

Harry

Chapter 20 the inverness nightmare

This was supposed to have been his new chance, new chance pffft, well look how that turned out. He was going to systematically avenge all the scum in this city who had wronged him. It takes Kevin a little under two hours to run to inverness, he is very careful to avoid being spotted , after all he had to keep this strange transformation a secret for now. He jumps across fields and streams like he's running over a Lego city in some child's dream.

Eventually he reaches an outskirt sign for the city of inverness, under the word inverness, the Gaelic for translation INHIMBIRNIS. He used to find this Scottish and quaint but now he couldn't give two fucks. The only thing on his mind now was finding those three little fucks from the bookmakers, they will suffer like they made him suffer oh boy they were going to make them suffer he must locate all three of the little pricks. He thinks, collect all of them individually, then take them somewhere isolated, somewhere to have a wee get together. His sanity is long gone, all rational thought is now clear but untainted with care or remorse. He looks down at his appearance, still tattered not good he thinks, must be dressed for my party with these three little fuckers. He walks in to the town a bit more hope for a clothes shop, so he can blend in a bit better and track them down. But then he stumbles upon is something better

a dry cleaner.

 Hmmm its open he thinks. The hunger he had felt before he had drunk from jo the hill walker was creeping back quickly and the need for human blood increasing. He looked through the window of the small, green dry cleaners there is a short, young boy probably about nineteen if he had to guess. The first point of choice since his change is here, can he cross the border between revenge and evil murder, yes, he had been killing the horrible people that had done wrong to him but could he kill an innocent? Fuck yeah, he could, well here we go, he thinks, time to cross that barrier. He pushes open the little green door that matches the shop front and a small bell dings, as it does the small chap looks up to see who has entered, a sudden feeling of concern floods over him when he sees that it is Kevin.

"hmmm can I help you?"

He dribbles out in fear

"Help well, you see, sorry what's your name?"

Kevin says

"Thomas "

He replies still on edge

"well you see Thomas I have a really good sense of smell these days so I can smell that you are all alone here and that there is nobody anywhere close "

There is a small tv playing in the background, the news was on is says in big letters

STV NEWSFLASH ANIMAL ATTACK LEAVES HIKERS MUTALATTED

"My dad is just at the bank he will be back any time soon "

Thomas said in concern

But Kevin's knew he was lying, he doesn't know how, it must be some kind of hunch but he just seems to know, He grabs the poor boy by the wrist, he lets out a yelp and tries to pull away but Kevin snaps his wrist, he goes to scream in agony but Kevin whips his hand over his mouth as he does blood starts to leak from his fingernail's digging into his face. His eyes ignite with water and they pour out of his young eyes. Kevin thinks, time to try the Hollywood neck thing, he lunges his teeth in to his neck, blood erupts like a water fountain, he sucks has hard and fast as he can, the blood runs down his throat touching every nerve on the way past. All his body comes to life even more than before. Thomas shakes and twitches, Kevin pulls away and drops his lifeless body to the ground like a disused, drained can of juice. He spits on him and turns to a large rack of hanging body shaped containers, he opens them one at a time shaking his head at each one but somewhere in the middle he stops

"ahhh yesses jackpot, ya dancer, ahhh baby"

He pulls out a long silk shirt purple in colour and a black pair of suede jeans, oh he falls in love immediately, he slides his hideous clothes off till he is completely naked, he notices there is no smell emanating from him anymore. He feels his skin smooth as a glass, no sweat at all. He slides his new clothes on, they fit like a glove, suddenly he feels a noise in his ear a voice, shit the wee fucker wasn't lying, there is a voice in the back room. Quick kill mode he thinks and flips over a desk and into the back room, his eyes scan left, right, nothing then they focus tight on an answering machine. What the hell.

It talks again

"Hi Thomas, its dad here I thought you might be away from the shop, just a wee message to let you know me and mum were going to stay a few more nights here in Madrid, just close up for a few days and go enjoy yourself with your pals, you're a good lad. love you son "

Kevin laughs, perfect he thinks, he grabs a pair of nice kahki coloured shoes and socks and slides them on, he moves to a small sink splashes cold water on his hair and throws it upon in a spikey fashion

At last the image he had always wanted. He walks out of the drycleaners, on the way out he drops the venetian blind and turns the

store sign to closed and snaps of the door handle. That's fixed that urge! Now back to the three skinny cunts who beat the shit out of Kevin. His plan is to terrorise the William hill worker by snapping his toes off one at a time until he has the location of every one of the teenagers address or hang outs. But when he arrives, in the distance, he cannot believe his new luck. All three of the little shits are outside the bookmakers smoking, oh sweet god this is so lucky, let's not waste this chance. He thinks carefully of strategy, after all a frontal attack and they could scatter. He holds back and follows these pricks, after about an hour of moving in and out of the bookies the eventually start to head off down the street. Kevin creeps carefully behind them in a stealth manner, like a jaguar moving in and out of passing opportunities and slowly analysing the behaviour of his prey, waiting on his chance to pounce. The sky turns black and raindrops begin to drop first one, then two, then hundreds, then thousands with each step getting more and more large in circumference. The pace of three teens hastens, then moves in to a park, a large sign at the entrance.
WHIN PARK

There is a large wooden fort styled building with a big metal snake slide lunging and coiling round it like an alien beast . The teens move under it to get shelter, Kevin moves into the darkness of the wood, he takes a position where he can here see and smell everything. He looks to the ground, there is a small rabbit eating grass, he stamps on it killing it instantly, the squelch dampened by the sound of the rain. The teens are none the wiser, they begin getting comfy in their new place of shelter. The teen with the blonde beard reaches into his pocket and pulls out a small pipe. He begins to pack it tightly with buds of plant cannabis. Kevin's nose tingles as he remembers this smell but now in such a different way. The urge to get wasted – gone! The need to bury his insecurities with alcohol and drugs – gone! He allows them to continue smoking as they pass the pipe around to each other smoking it on several puffs each. Eventually, boredom sets in. He picks up a small stone the size of marble and launches it to the metal slide. It makes a large reverberating noise that echoes throughout the whole park. The teens immediately freak out and grab the pipe and place it into the nearest pocket. The teen with the black jacket and yellow compass moves out to investigate, as the other two hides cautiously behind him. Kevin runs rapidly at his full new speed, he floats past the teen ripping out his eye on the way past. He repeats the motion in reverse motion and takes the other eye. This whole motion takes no more than four seconds and is invisible to the human eye. Behind him the teen with the dark blonde beard says

"Woooaah Stevo – What the fuck was that? Are you ok man?"

But as Stevo turns around, both other teens fall back in horror and shock! As dark red blood trickles down where his eyes used to be. Now realising what has happened to him, Stevo screams to the highest of his voice in terror. The screams fill the air in the night like a horror movie climax. The two friends fall backwards and begin to scatter. The teen with the blonde beard turns to run, as he does a hand meets him. It punches him so hard, breaking all his ribs, he tries to scream but nothing comes out. He falls to the ground in agony and starts writhing. The last teen now witnessing this, tries to run in the opposite direction, but as he goes to take off, he is met by the confrontational Kevin. He immediately turns to runs the opposite direction. There is a hissing noise, and to his disbelief Kevin is now waiting on the other side of him. The teen falls to his knees and starts sobbing, Kevin looks at him, He doesn't realise why but he had labelled the teen with the torn-out eyes as the ring leader of this fuckwit group,. he whispers in the sobbing teens ear.

"if you move an inch, I'll kill, you just wait here, and everything will be ok "

Kevin leaves the sobbing teen and heads over to the dark blond bearded, one he lies on the ground spitting blobs of blood from his mouth, they land in his beard melting in like quicksand. The same process occurs on his woven green jumper, blobs of his blood tricking into the crisscross fibre as well. He looks up towards Kevin as he skips across in a comical manor.

"hi there little one, remember# beating me in to a pulp, you really hurt my ribs, hmm looks like I've returned the favour"

the teen looks in horror as he tries to work out how the little junkie they beat up and robbed is repaired and overpowering them. He looks to his sobbing friend who is contemplating running again but is too immobilized by fear. This is only reinforced by that fact Kevin rolls up the sleeve of his new shirt and smashes his hand in to the bearded teens head. His hand sinks in to his face like a Christmas pudding, even Kevin's new strength surprises him as he meets soft soil on the other side instead of brain and bone. The face of the one remaining teen turns the colour of white paint. He bends to the side and is violently sick, he watches in complete terror as Kevin withdraws his hand and washes it in a nearby puddle The teen is sick once again, this time onto himself, he looks for aid but only can see the rain washing blood from the eye sockets of his friend and the head of his other friend filling up like a mug. He covers his face, this is all a dream, he thinks this cannot be real, must be that acid he took at the weekend. He uncovers one eye, he cannot see Kevin oh good he thinks, he might have spared me, might have shown mercy on me, please please let this be the case. He suddenly feels a tap to his shoulder he turns slowly and is met by a smiling Kevin

"didn't think I forgot about you did I little piggy "

Kevin says gently

He flips the teen on to his front the fear returns and the sobbing begins again

"we were poor, I'm sorry we didn't know you "

"I care for my poor mum, I'm all she has, please she will die without me "

The excuses keep pouring out the teens mouth but Kevin couldn't care less he peels off the teen's shoes and socks and lift's him onto his knees with his feet facing back

"now about these little piggy's, hope you're not ticklish"

Before the teen even answers, Kevin breaks his small toe while holding him, he still he screams in agony. Kevin breaks another and then another until his toes are left and right stacked like pencils hanging out of a mug, the teen tries to crawl away in a pathetic manner, Kevin slides over to his front

"Ohno no no, there are still ten little piggies' left "

Kevin says, while looking at his fingers

"noooooooooooo noooooooooooooo noooooooooooooo ahhh pppllleeeeeeeaaaaasaseeee noooooooooooooo"

Sick is coming and going now from his mouth in-between the gasps for air, in between the pain. Kevin grabs his hand the teen moves in and out of terrifying consciousness as Kevin breaks all his fingers, then forearms and shins, the now apposable teen snapped at all joints looks up to Kevin and says

"please kill me"

Kevin looks at him

"oh, ok I suppose so I really have a lot of people to see tonight. Now that the teen cannot move Kevin grasps in to the soft ground and pulls a large pile of soft soil and lays it over his head he tries to resist, he probably thought he was just going to get his neck snapped or face demolished. This was much worse Kevin lays several small piles over his face leaving him suffocating slowly and waits till he can longer hear his heartbeat. He then spends his next hour collecting large slabs of rocks and stones and forcing them into the trouser pockets, and any other way possible on the teenagers bodies . Once he's filled every place, he launches their bodies in to a small lake in the immediate area, there bodies float for a second and then begin to bubble, then descend in to the darkness. Kevin knows this will not hide them for long, but he didn't need long he didn't need long at all ! He was working through his list quite efficiently, he skips away laughing and humming in-between breaths , he heads into the town, there was a little security guard he was wanting a word with ….

Chapter 21 The ape

Uhamish is a man of very little needs, he needs his god, and his wife, these two things coupled with his job, oh yea and he loves lifting weights, it's like a passion for him. As a Muslim he shouldn't really use drugs, but he cannot live without his muscle and weight. His mind still clouded by all the beatings he took in school, also being referred to as the skinny god boy, or the filthy coon. There was no respect, so Uhamish would build himself up like a train and gain their respect, this was his plan. After school he hit the gym with every spare moment but with each passing day seeing very little results. He prayed hard to Allah in the hope of divine intervention he had no success so after years of trying fads and protein shakes, he was met by Phil the local man at the gym who sells three syringes of steroids for £120. This ate a lot of money from Uhamish family but there was no reason why he could not be the muscle tank he wanted to be. Forget his wife and his god, they would forgive him he thought. So he now meets Phil once a week and on his lunch break he goes to the staff toilet in Primark and injects his hand with Deca Durabolin and then after work hits the gym for a few hours before enjoying a nice curry, loyally made by his wife Kasmia, This was his life, his routine. He sits behind the two glass doors of Primark beside the pull up lace baskets (you know the ones). He grunts at everybody that passes in different context, some a small dismissal of a grunt, almost a goodbye and some a snarling large grunt to evoke fear in case they were shoplifters. He sat there every day sometimes he would patrol the store, but the steroids have many side effects, one main one was a tight feeling in his upper legs. This, of course, meant pursuing assailants was limited to close combat, so guarding the exit made sense. Sometimes he gets a radio call from another worker in the store, but he must fight through the pain and chase down a young prick trying to get handy. But most of the time he was known to locals as the door monkey, due to the fact that the steroids had swelled his hands to massive proportions, in fact he couldn't remember the last time he had seen his penis erect. This was an uneventful day he was waiting at the door picking objects from his nostril and eating them. Then Kevin walks into the store and smiles at the beast. He looks bamboozled for a second, he must stare for another second, yes it was him! nobody ever comes back after he has banned them. It just doesn't happen, steroid rage bursts into full force

"WHAT THE FUCK ARE YOU DOING YOU ARE BANNNEEED "

He screams in Kevin's face

"if I'm banned ape boy how can I do this "

As Kevin says this, he picks up the container holding all the net bags and launches it into a rack of jeans, the guard turns into a bull and charges at Kevin. Almost instantly Kevin, using his new speed side steps it with ease and the monkey guard crashes into another rack of cheap Chinese assembled dresses. Like a bird in custard, he waves around flapping, throwing dresses left right and centre. After freeing himself from the dress custard his eyes ignite again in steroid rage, he charges after Kevin

"c'mon fatty "

Kevin says   taunting him and then runs up an escalator while the beast is in hot pursuit. Kevin makes it all the way into a door labelled

STAFF ROOM.

Along a white corridor with no ceiling, just vents and airducts like open guts of some mighty metal beast. He leaves the guard searching through the store, enters the staff room, as he enters, he walks in and there is a young lad sitting there drinking a tea and fig rolls. He looks at Kevin confused

"oh hi, can I help you "

The young guy says helpfully

Kevin doesn't even speak he snaps his neck like a twig, he made a grunt noise then dies. Kevin sighs, this little prick is ruining all the surprise, he grabs the body over his shoulder and pushes through a smaller door he is met by two blue toilet cubicles, he slumps the young guy up on one of the toilets and closes the door, he bends the lock in place so it can't be opened. He is about to climb up into the ceiling tiles when two things in the room catch his attention. Firstly, a television in the corner the giving a news report

"so, this is Suzanne Bergan from stv news, it has been a sad day for inverness, a bus driver has died, and it has not been said yet what caused the crash that left no passengers dead. Friends of Mr harry Denver report he had been heavily intoxicated the night before the crash and that the amount he had consumed could have never been out his system by the time of the accident, Crews are still trying to reach the bus and salvage any evidence but it plunged over two hundred meters and there is not much to go on right now we will keep you updated as soon as we have more ...and now the weather .... "

Kevin smiles for a second as he remembers as clear as crystal Harry's demise. But then back to the job on hand. The other thing he had noticed was a bag, and his new nose could smell it was an identical scent to the security guard. He reaches in, its full of micro syringes all 10ml, perfect he thinks as he swirls up in to the ceiling tiles. He waits and he waits, and finally the guard enters the main room

"you must be in here I've checked the whole store and have the exits covered, come out now and I will limit you to seventeen punches "

He spits out of his steroid inflamed mouth

Kevin sniggers

The guard monkeys around the room checking everywhere, he looks at the bathroom door and smiles

"got you little CUNT"

He says while kicking open the door. To his shock there is no one there but one of the cubicles is closed. He stands at the door and shoves, but nothing happens, he pushes with his ape strength the door flies open,

"asrggggggg got y---oo---uu......."

He realises that he hasn't grabbed Kevin but that of his dead work mate! He falls backward as the realisation kicks in. As He stands Kevin drops from the ceiling slapping the back of his head and forcing Uhamish to fall forward landing on his dead college. He lies on top of the dead human boy for a second before climbing back to his feet. Kevin laughs out loud, the beast is angered, Kevin lets him take a punch, it feels like a drop of water landing on Kevin's face, the guard takes several more hits into Kevin's face. He looks up gasping, not a mark, what the hell he thinks, he looks at the ground the broken door has a wooden splint like a small dagger, he grabs it and lunges it into Kevin's neck. This surprises Kevin, he spurts blood out his mouth, its drips all over his new shirt. The guard stands and looks smug, he had beaten this criminal and won. Time to call the police on this murdering bastard. he turns expecting to see the now dead Kevin but instead he is standing looking very cross indeed.

"look what the fuck you just done to my new shirt you CUNT, his eyes turn black as the night "

Kevin screams at the ape

The ape screams back in terror

"WHAT THE HELL ARE YOU "

Kevin doesn't answer he didn't deserve words anymore after ruining Kevin's new shirt. He pulls the piece of wood out his neck, it drips further blood on his shirt. He feels the wound on his neck, there are similar strings like he seen on the river object connecting his neck back together and knitting it in a matter of seconds, his neck is now repaired. Watching this fills Uhamish with fear, now he knew no matter what steroids he used or how many years he lifted weights he could never beat this foe. Kevin forces the wood through Uhamish shoulder and in to the toilet door he doesn't scream, that surprises Kevin he just releases a dark grunt, then looks at Kevin in anger, grunting furiously in his direction Kevin reaches in to his bag and pulls out a handful of Uhamish's Deca Durabolin syringes, he smiles at him, as he grunts and now looks concerned. Kevin gently pushes one in his shoulder then another even thou it was illegal. He was still very set only one every three days. Uhamish feels a rush of adrenaline, his heart start beating and he get a rush of flutters in his eyes and finger tips, he looks at Kevin in further rage but stuck quite firmly bleeding out to the toilet cubicle Kevin injects him with another, this time pain rushes in to his chest and his eyes go white for a second. Each time Kevin injects him he is leaving the syringe's in as well. he uses another this time, as he does Uhamish lets out a scream as the pain shoots body wide, his heart is not racing any more but now pounding in agony. Kevin goes to inject him again but this time he starts shaking his head at him.

"nono pleacchee nnoo mooooreeh"

he says, His words now slurred

Kevin sticks the next one in his head and depresses the syringe, something bursts inside Uhamish's eye socket, the pain is unreal he screams, and dark blood engulfs his eye and he loses vision. He suffers a small stroke known as a TIA, his arm becomes numb and he gets massive pain in his leg he can't even feel his feet now, he tries to focus on Kevin, he sees him holding the last five syringes. Kevin stabs all five into his chest and screams, the pain explodes, all moving in to Uhamish heart then he is met by strange sensation of being alive while you know your heart has stopped. He tries to breathe but with each breath darkness creeps closer and his mind becomes fuzzy, Kevin smiles and watches him die. He moves out the toilet, no way he could hide this one. He moves back into the corridor there is a door labelled,

STOCK

He slides into a room of opportunity, he picks the nicest shirt Primark can offer and discards his old one and slides into the new one then, he leaves the building via an emergency fire exit. Carefully avoiding being seen he re-enters the world, Time to leave Inverness, he thinks, the heat will be on him now. He doesn't care what happens to him after this murder spree, but he must complete his task he walks with haste towards the train station, then into the restroom, there is a man in a suit washing his hands. Kevin smiles at him the man he smiles back, he opens the disabled cubicle, smashes the man's face off the sink and drags him into the it. He reaches into his pockets takes a wallet and leaves a pager and cigarettes, the man starts to grumble, fuck he was still alive. Kevin holds his mouth and nose shut with one hand and starts peeling open the wallet with the other, he takes a wad of cash from it, as the man suffocates and dies. It doesn't phase Kevin at all he wanders out whistling looking carefully not to be spotted by anyone. He Goes Straight to the window to buy a ticket.

"Good morning, darling, one ticket to Edinburgh one-way PLEASE"

he says before the woman even notices him, she looks up and smiles, she taps away at the keyboard and a small printer prints a ticket.

"There you are sir, thirty-six pounds please", he smiles back, thanks the woman and heads to the train departures board, its big yellow words state

EDINBURGH 15:05

He finds his train, gets his seat and closes his eyes and as opposed to the drug fuelled ride on the way up, he no longer felt tired he no longer ,he needed to sleep, he just closed his eyes and felt he could relive anything he wanted like a rerun of a movie. He sat for most of the journey reliving the time since he left Glencoe and contemplating what he now was and how it had come to be. Although he was enjoying every moment of this revenge spree there was still the question of how it happened? And that was eating away at him, the curiosity at some point would need to be satisfied.

He arrives at the Haymarket station, a miniature Edinburgh station like a small hub just before the main one, Waverley station. He looks out the window as the train railroads his life in reverse, he sees areas he knows well fly past at high speed, all these things seem almost like remnants of a different life. He considers killing one of the passengers as he needs the urge of hunger under control, as the next victim was nearby he wanted no distractions, no problems, he would need a distraction as well to keep the old boys in blue distracted while he took care of the potato shop owner Then he remembered the pub staff that had rejected him and called him a fuckin junkie. Oh yes, that would be the perfect distraction oh yes, that's the one he thinks, grinning. He waits for his train to arrive, living a few more memories on the way. At last, Waverly station, but he still needed some blood to help clear his mind when he turns the corner, he realises there is a massive police presence in the courtyard of the station. About eight officers, one with a machine gun strapped to his side, he leans back pretending to read a sign and focus his ears towards them.

"Right keep eye on everyone who disembarks! Somebody killed two people in Inverness station, I want you to check each and every one of these folks and vet them as you go, there's a chance that they're still in Inverness, it looks like a robbery but there has been some mutilation and what appears to be some form of cult behaviour so check all of them "

Shit, Kevin can't get stopped yet and he's not quite sure what bullets will do to him, yet he's quite sure they won't kill him, but they probably will slow him down. He looks back at the train, it's about to leave and head back to Haymarket and then on to Glasgow. Kevin jumps back on to the train, he stands in the door area and waits, the windows in this train can be pulled down, so just he sits and waits patiently. The train whistle goes on the platform and the train starts to move, Kevin's plan is to jump from the moving train almost as soon as it leaves. He lowers the single pane of glass down, he can hear a slow engaging intricacy of gears and metal moving, he sticks his head out and formulates his plan … Suddenly a tap on his shoulder? What the hell? He turns around and sees a small man dressed in blue uniform, wearing perfectly round glasses and black side swept hair almost like a little fresh Hitler but in a more train way!

"yes "

Kevin says

"you left this train in Edinburgh so how can you have bought a new ticket to Glasgow already? Ehh? train skipping is a very serious offence, I suggest you pay the fare now and we can leave this matter alone "

the small Hitler says, almost sounding like a recording from the train company, Kevin looks at him for a second almost astounded that this little man had any balls at all. He smiles

"I will pay the fare but there only one small condition "

Kevin says calmly

The small Hitler looks confused

"what is the condition "

He reply's

"you fix the mess in that bathroom, it's horrible"

Wait he thinks, there no mess, he checks these bathrooms like clockwork! Trains were his life almost as much as being efficient, he flips round in a haste and throws the bathroom door open. It is such a light door he just about rips it off the handle as it opens. He is presented by an immaculate bathroom so clean you could eat food in there. He smiles his glasses begin steaming from the rage.

 ahhh yes, he thinks, perfect and clean, he is confused? Why was this little kid trying to say his bathroom is a mess? Is this some kind of prank played by other colleagues? Hmm he is about to turn to see what the little shit has to say for himself, before he does, he feels something touch his neck, he goes to touch it to see what it is. He feels another face pressed up against him then two intense bee stings on his neck. He tries to jump forward, then back but it's to late, something has him. Kevin drains all blood from his body, it gets dark and the poor conductor dies, Kevin closes the door of the toilet leaving him in there and then speaks a thought out loud,

"wait a minute why the fuck is everybody I kill ending up in bathrooms ha ha"

He shrugged his shoulders

"defiantly the next two no bathrooms ha-ha"

He climbs into the window space and gets ready to jump, the trains now moving at some speed and in a long tunnel. Stupid conductor, wasting time but also, he saved the job of getting blood before the potato worker, just a distraction needed now! He jumps trying to get the best landing ever but that fails, he lands side on with a post breaking his hip and arm, then running his face through gravel, he lies for a few minutes feeling his face push out the gravel and his body crack internally as it seems to repair itself, He was truly a legend a creature from origin not television, the things from history and folklore. He gets to his feet, shakes his clothes down. Right he really needed to get a move on, time was short, potato man would soon be gone till tomorrow. He runs his new speed to the pub, when he arrives, he investigates the window. Its higher than he can see, he hops easily about a metre if the ground twice and sees the two barmen working and talking but no customers.

BASTARDS, he thinks, he strolls causally in the pub, the two men look at him instantly.

"shit, they think, not him again"

They talk

"look you are barred, we don't want any trouble but if you don't leave there will be trouble, we will call the police "

Kevin does not look impressed

"LET ME FUCKING SEE; YOU DON'T OFFER ME A JOB "

He picks up an ashtray and throws it at full speed through the phone on the wall.

"YOU FUCKING MOCK ME, CALL ME WHAT WAS IT? OH, YEA A JUNKIE CUNT "

He picks up another ashtray and throws it in to the gleaming whiskey display behind them. the bottles explode spraying alcohol everywhere like a slow-motion glass explosion. the both cover their head

"I DON'T HAVE MUCH TIME OR I WOULD MAKE YOU TWO LITTLE PRICKS SUFFER MORE "

Kevin launches about three more ashtrays smashing nearly every other bottle, he walks up to the bar

The two men stunned by the explosions, rise to see what happened but Kevin is waiting holding a pink lighter he had lifted from the bar

"got a light "?

Kevin says while smiling.

 The two men look at each other and turn white as the broken glass
and mixture of whisky saturate their bodies. Kevin lays the lighter
down on the bar and strikes, to his surprise it lights first time and a
low, light blue flame veers off in the direction of the two men, they
try and run but there is no hope, they both ignite first in blue then
bright yellow. Kevin turns to walks out and as he does all the bar is
adorned with the screams of the two burning men. He walks out and
moves a wee bit up the street and screams at the top of his voice

"ohhh my god, fire, this pub is on FIRE"

Several people run in to nearby phone boxes and call 999. Suddenly a
fire ball explodes out of the pub and the windows smash across the
entire road, Kevin looks at the blaze

"holy shit wow "

He had never blown up anything before, that was impressive. In a
matter of an hour there is eight fire engines, two ambulances and an
array of police cars. in the distance a small potato shop is blocked by
smoke and fire engines a small man peers over the chaos trying to see
what'd happening,

But unsuspecting to him Kevin has his dark black eyes locked on him
......

Chapter 22 The capital

Antonio was a potato worker, all he knew was every way on this gods earth how to cook potatoes, his father was a potato worker and his grandfather before him there was no other way to say it, he is a potato man. His shop bright red and neatly tucked away into Edinburgh's old town. He supplies the local market for three generations. He had never doubted himself ever! He had never had a complaint, he also monopolized the market in the local office field, all the workers placed orders and his nephew had been delivering them for the past five years, but his nephew had new ideas, he wanted to go work in Zante in Greece and be a manager of his own night club. He was young and Antonio had no kids so the thought had crossed his mind that his nephew would succeed him. But that was all over now with, each passing day Antonio had been getting more depressed, he thought it couldn't get any worse until his nephew had announced that he was leaving in four weeks. This crushed poor Antonio as that left him little time to find a replacement, and with time creeping in he would lose all his new office contracts. He was too old to run all those errands himself and who would watch the shop? He put a notice up in the shop window in the hope of getting some eighteen-year-old student with tight breasts and a short skirt to help but instead a collection of all the city morons and wasters, one even smashed up his shop and had to be arrested. No things weren't going well for him at all. He was at a low point already when his friend that night in the pub insinuated that due to his receding hairline and dark-skinned forehead that he was becoming a potato himself. Antoni did not find this amusing in the slightest, he threw his pint all over his friend who was shocked by this, as Antonio was normally the most placid man in the universe but everything combined and then being referred to as a human potato was just enough, he leaves his friend dripping with beer and heads back to his little shop to mourn. He sits down on his little white stool that has always been there since his grandfather, and thinks what the "fuck am I going to do"

there is no one out there he puts his head onto his knees and sobs quietly

"GRANPA WHAT WOULD YOU DO? "

He shouts at his feet.

He sniffs, hmmm, something is burning he sniffs deeper this time lifting his head, what the hell something is on fire? He jumps and checks all his appliances in his kitchen then both potato ovens, nope nothing. He looks around then he sees people moving quickly past the shop window, he moves out through the shop counter and opens his front door. He peers out, the pub on the corner is smoking, he nips back in and calls 999 but they say some one is already on the way. He heads back out to watch as he does, a fire ball implodes from the building and black smoke bellows out as it rocks the street.

Antonio was not going to worry about this, his shop was out of reach, this might also buy him some time. He calls his friend to see if he's alright, he stays across from the pub, thank god he had gone home and is now watching the blaze from his window.

"yea the two barmen, Gary and Tommy were still in I think they're trying to fight through the blaze now, but I hear they had hundreds of bottles of whisky in storage under the bar and that's like a petrol bomb. The power was cut an hour. ago I don't know how long till we lose the pho,,,,,,,,,,,,,,,,,,,,eeeeeeeeeeeeeeeeeeeeeeeeeeeeeeeeeeeeeeeeeeeeeeeee e"

And the phone cuts off in Antonio's hand, he turns the receiver round to his face and looks at it as if his look will repair it, he sighs and hangs back up the receiver. He heads back out to watch the blaze, he stands leaning against his shop talking to the occasional passer-by, but it gets quiet as they cordon off the area and as the blaze intensifies. Antonio thinks time to shut up the shop and get home, he is about to turn around and head back in to close when he gets a strong feeling of being watched. He turns around to look past the sirens and crackling of the fire there is a set of eyes, a familiar set of eyes, the young boy that has smashed up his shop.

"Fuck "

He whispers

 he turns around to renter his shop when an intense gust of wind rushes past him in a whirling motion. He looks back and Kevin is gone, there is no one there? He hurries into the shop and bolts the door. The police would take too long to get to him tonight with all this fire. and he had just got his shop back together he locks the door and double checks it a final time

"ah all secure and safe"

As he says this suddenly a feeling of deep dread fills him, he was not alone! But how could any one have got past him? His shop has no back door, he was very confused, he turns around slowly and is met by a tidied-up version of Kevin sitting on his family stool picking his teeth with a toothpick. They stare at each other for a second, the rage fills Antonio's eyes ...

"get out my shop NOW, how dare you, little cunt I'll kill you "

He flies towards Kevin with the intent of killing him with whatever he could reach but as he reaches Kevin he takes a small step forward and slaps Antonio's forehead with might, rendering him unconscious in one shot, his potato head hits the wooden floor like a sack of spuds. He feels no pain, no knockout effect just immediate darkness in instant. Time passes, then some more, eventually Antonio begins to regain his ability to see. The first thing he sees is the roof of his shop fuzzy, but yes defiantly his ceiling , he had been looking at it for years he knew it well, as his vision clears he looks around, he seems to be tied in several points to his counter. He looks at his left hand and foot, they are the only ones that can move slightly, stretched out in full length. He trembles and peers into the darkness of his powerless shop. Kevin is standing wearing one of his sanitary masks and pushing a small metal table towards him. On it a large metal contraption, he gulps, it was his meat slicer! He tries to talk but realises he has been gagged

"nnmmmmmmmmmmmm"

He mumbles at Kevin

Kevin looks at him for a second then talks.

"I have just one very important question for you "

The mumbling stops and Antonio stares at him in desperate interest

"this defiantly isn't a bathroom or toilet, right?"

Antonio looks even more confused and terrified

"WELL IS IT, "

he screams in his face Antonio, he shakes his head rapidly.

"well good, I've really been trying to change the theme of this evening to something other than bogs and lavatories "

he says in humour. Antonio starts to let what tears he has left flow out his eyes, Kevin looks pathetically at him.

"I'm going to remove your gag if you scream, I will slap you again and we start this all over again "

Antonio nods in agreeance and Kevin removes his gag. before he even has a chance to talk Kevin begins.

"I had done nothing to you, why didn't you want to help me?"

He looks at him intensely.

Now this surprises Kevin, Antonio spits in his face

"you didn't have what it takes. this is my family business and you're just a worthless piece of shit "

That's it, finally Antonio has cracked, this had been months in the making, but that was it, game over. He's done, no more mental health to give! Kevin still amazed by his outburst wipes his face

"WORTHLESS FUCKING WORTHLESS well let's just see then "

He smiles evilly at him and refits the gag. He pulls the machine closer and kicks an on button at the base, it whirls into action, not buzzing like most metal contraptions, but more a whirring noise like two knifes rubbing together. He opens an empty potato container and pretends to start mixing an invisible potato with a fork.

"Hi sir, how can I help you?"

Kevin directs at an invisible shop customer. Antonio stares to the invisible location and looks confused

"ahh yes sir, so you would like salt and butter "

He empties invisible butter in with an immaculate knife, then sprinkles fake salt"

Antonio watches completely confounded

"ah ok yea we can do that…… two hundred slices of potato shop worker"

Antonio turns white, he looks at Kevin as he does Kevin grabs his hand holding it still while Kevin's foot moves the machine closer, and closer. First the finger tops go , then fore finger , he muffles screams through his gag his eyes searching for sanity and saviour, the pain intensifies as he slices him cm at a time, in a matter of minutes his fingers are disks of flesh and bone lying on the floor. You think that would be enough for Kevin. Wrong, he looks up to the counter.

"ah yes so you liked that so much you want another THOUSAND slices no fucking problem!!"

Antonio shakes his head while tears pour down his face, Kevin forces the machine towards him quickly eradicating his arm in seconds Blood splatters across his face and he screams at Antonio, as he does Antonio feels things go distant, , he feels tired as the blood pours from his arm socket.

The generations have ended, Antonio dies! Kevin sucks blood from his arm socket and savours every inch. Once Kevin has had his fill, he wipes his face on Antonio's apron then spits in his face and sniggers in evil. As the burning pub embers and flames light up the exterior window glowing off his face like an orange kaleidoscope he smiles.

He and heads off now to have a we chat with Davies girl, then physically pull her head from her body while her still alive, as he leaves his new ears are filled by the crackling embers of the burning pub. As he walks away this distraction of flickering noise has led him to miss the police officer that is sitting watching that end of the street has watched Kevin leaving the potato shop with what looks like blood on him.

Chapter 23 MORTEM

Kevin begins moving down the royal mile leaving the shop behind him but unknown to him, the police officer has just entered the shop to see if everything is ok. He pokes his head in the shop.

"hello Police, everything ok "

As he says this, he sees the mangled mess of a corpse of Antonio, he falls back in pure and utter shock as he scrambles back to his car. he holds down a button on shoulder,

"white male dark hair white tee-shirt. code 445, armed and extremely dangerous. Armed response unit required suspect on foot, leaving Worlds End pub moving down royal mile. The officer is then sick as he can't shake the image of poor Antonio, he climbs into his car and leaves the armed response to their job.

Kevin skips in a comical manner, he is thinking long and hard about the pain and conflict he is going to cause and, in his brain, creating a list of all people that had wronged him in his life and who would also pay under his new powers. Suddenly his shoulder implodes in agony, the first real pain he's felt since Glencoe. He has been shot! He looks at his shoulder, there is a large red wound dripping with blood desperately trying to instantly heal. He turns around slowly, there are three well armoured police officers moving gradually towards him pointing machine guns at him, he laughs.

"Only three of you scary wooooaaa"

He rushes towards the left officer pushing his hand in to his chest, killing him instantly. The other officers jump back in fear and astonishment but as Kevin goes to rush the second officer he is filled by an array of bullets. They enter his body in quick succession from both other machine guns. They stop firing, Kevin sits on the ground crouched, at least thirty bullets in different locations of his body, he feels a weakness that moves over him.

Shit, he thinks these guys might win! Maybe he wasn't as invincible as he thought. He looks down the street, as the officers look in astonishment at the fact Kevin is still alive, another two police cars are moving up the street

"fuck this "

Kevin mumbles. He uses all strength that remains and channels it into his speed and whips away in a flash, further confusing the two remaining officers. He manages to run to a crossroads, there is a chemist on the one corner, but he walks past it, there a small lane, he moves down it to seek refuge. As he is going down the stone winding alley, he sees a doorway, already he can smell the human urine after years of abuse by the junkies that frequent this lane. He falls to the ground while he feels his body expel the bullets and knit back together, he lies writhing in pain

"ok so bullets don't bounce off me "

he says out loud as he heals. It takes about twenty-five minutes to fully heal. He stands to his feet and looks at his tee-shirt and pokes his fingers through the bullet holes. Wow, he thinks, that was close he was nearly caught, they might have turned him in to some kind of lab experiment. Suddenly he feels a strong feeling of emptiness, like he was just a hollow skin costume that contains nothing but air. his steps become heavier like quicksand, a wave of thirst hits the back of his throat. He stumbles then he then realises what's wrong

BLOOD HE NEEDS MORE BLOOD!

This was a horrible sensation like having pebbles glued to your skin. He runs down the staircase twitching all the way to the bottom as he does, he collides with someone. He looks up it's the police officer that found Antonio. Although Kevin didn't know him, he clearly new Kevin. the officer tries to stumble back away in fear, reaching for a baton. Kevin lunges at him and sinks his teeth deep in to his chest, the officer feels blood trickle down his perfectly ironed shirt, white, blending with deep red. The blood travels at a rate of knots into Kevin. Each step the police officers' pulse is getting weaker. He dies in agony no happy ending here! Kevin punches his fist in to a stone brick wall, assembled by ancient flag stones, it implodes into dust

"gggggggrrrr aaa why has this happened to me what am I? I need answers "

He turns slowly round behind him to see the plaque, Waverly station

YES, back to the scene where all this weirdness began. He will investigate maybe he will find his own rotting body with its wrists cut, alarming him to the fact this might be purgatory and all this a test of his good and evil nature, oh god he thinks. He looks over the bridge to scope for police.

"fuck"

 he whispers, there are four officers scouring, the station, he can see the Inverness train it's about to leave. He leaps over the wall and lands on the tracks, he looks carefully around and starts creeping towards the back of the train. He sees his opportunity a double-sided luggage carriage left unattended, he leaps forward and lands in it. He finds a small metal cupboard for bikes clips it open and reverses in, he pulls the door shut to only leave his dark eyes visible in a strap missing from the door. He waits train Quietly for the whistle blow. the carriage shuts and he feels movement, the train rumbles and moves but all Kevin can think about is what he will find there in the mystery glen? Dead Kevin? Superhero serum? Radiation? All sci-fi movies burst in his head at once, but he was none the wiser. He finally arrives and waits for the train to be completely emptied and waits a further thirty minutes just to be safe. Then he starts walking Quickly right past the toilet crime scene, right out the station right past the Primark, faster walking, still faster, faster past the drycleaner out on to the A82 road. Suddenly he is running, time stops and ceases to exist he notices Harrys last location with blue and white police tape. He starts to focus like he has never known, it sprays out him like a forcefield. He reaches Glencoe, stops stares around, he walks past the location of the campers and continues up the long winding road, through the shrub and into the glen. He stands and looks slowly from left to right, well no dead Kevin face down in the river, no aliens or plutonium. He starts searching the glen for clues. He looks in the moss for weird alien worms, he taps trees and lifts big rocks nope nothing, he screams into the air.

"WHAT THE FUCK ARE YOUUUUUU!!!!"

Then a realisation bursts in his mind like a fireball, the flake that had entered his mouth was travelling downstream. He whips his vision to the water fall, it was flowing hard but there was a wall behind it, he climbs and jumps up to the top of the fall, he looks for a second then grabs a fallen tree log and redirects the steam that feeds the water fall a couple of meters to the left. He scrambles he quickly scrambles down the glen, he looks at the wall behind the waterfall

"NOTHING "

He screams, he then takes a huge smell of the wall, the smell, oh god the smell! He almost falls back, the stench is unbearable. Death mixed with puss and slime and add some smallpox and you have this smell! Kevin grabs a stick and starts chiselling the wall. Something starts to become visible a small wooden square, strange? He thinks ahh, it's the end of a crate he rushes with excitement, after he chisels further a word in red becomes visible, he stands back and reads it out loud

"MORTEM (Latin for death)"

THE END
to be continued…………….

Printed in Great Britain
by Amazon